Mary, I hope you can find a piece of Key West you know in The story.

Fair winds & following seas...

CHASIN' THE WIND

MICHAEL HASKINS

FIVE STAR

A part of Gale, Cengage Learning

GALE
CENGAGE Learning™

Detroit • New York • San Francisco • New Haven, Conn • Waterville, Maine • London

Copyright © 2008 by Michael Haskins.

The Pilgrim: Chapter 33. Words and Music by Kris Kristofferson.

© 1970 (Renewed 1998) RESACA MUSIC PUBLISHING CO. All Rights Controlled and Administered by EMI BLACKWOOD MUSIC INC. All Rights Reserved. International Copyright Secured. Used by Permission.

Five Star Publishing, a part of Gale, Cengage Learning.

Set in 11 pt. Plantin.

Printed on permanent paper.

LIBRARY OF CONGRESS CATALOGING-IN-PUBLICATION DATA

Haskins, Michael.
    Chasin' the wind : a Mad Mick Murphy mystery / Michael Haskins. — 1st ed.
        p. cm.
    ISBN-13: 978-1-59414-638-1 (alk. paper)
    ISBN-10: 1-59414-638-1 (alk. paper)
    1. Journalists—Fiction. 2. Key West (Fla.)—Fiction. 3. Havana (Cuba)—Fiction. 4. United States—Relations—Cuba—Fiction. 5. Cuba—United States—Relations—Fiction. 6. Political fiction. I. Title.
    PS3608.A84C48 2008
    813'.6—dc22   2007041332

First Edition. First Printing: March 2008.

Published in 2008 in conjunction with Tekno Books and Ed Gorman.

Printed in the United States of America
1 2 3 4 5 6 7 12 11 10 09 08

DEDICATION

When I write there are ghosts with me, whispering encouragement, and messing with dialogue.

For those who couldn't wait around, who silently point out the good and the bad, who believed in me, I give my thanks, especially to my son, Sean Michael, my brother Danny; both were always proud of me. For my mother and father, Rose and Bill, who encouraged me to write, and my Aunt Peggy and Uncle Dick; she showed me that learning was an experience to be enjoyed; and he taught me to be proud of my Irish heritage and to enjoy a good story. For Aunt Harriet and Uncle Stan, who showed me a world I would have missed otherwise. And, for Dennis Lynds, who gave his support and encouragement from the first day we met in a bookstore more than twenty-five years ago.

Thank you for leaving me the memories, I miss you.

Then, of course, I have goblins hiding around my life, setting examples that are impossible to live up to; pranksters who make me laugh; voices of reason in moments of insanity; those responsible for my happiness. Many have affected my life, but none more than my sister, Patty Bolter. Her example of living and loving life, family, and friends far exceeds anything I can obtain, but I try. Then there's Seanan and Chela, my twin daughters, whose smiles light up my life like volcanic eruptions; I cannot imagine life without them, their laughter, and love.

I owe a special thanks to fellow Bostonian and writer Jeremiah Healy, whose years of encouragement and friendship have been priceless. I couldn't ask for a better sailing crew than Jerry.

And, to Tom Corcoran, a fellow Key West writer and scoundrel, who taught me patiently the importance of the first few pages.

Thanks to the gang of MWA's Florida Chapter writers who yelled their support long before I saw light at the end of the tunnel.

And last, but not least, to Celine and Alex for being special. Thank you!

ONE

The Key West Sail Club's small Sunfish and Laser sailboats bobbed in the breeze, their masts swaying, as I eased my dinghy next to the weathered dock. The warm, salty air came in off the Gulf Steam, blown across the Florida Straits from Cuba, carrying the scent of seaweed, hinting of tropical flora and rain.

I tied off the line and walked toward the clubhouse. The gate was open and Tom Hunter's motorcycle stood in the parking lot making ticking sounds as it cooled, but I didn't hear the radio or smell brewing coffee.

An old sail bag lay crumpled in the marl and tidal mud, an odd sight for a shipshape operation. Then the bag moaned.

Tom's face was crushed raw like pulverized meat, his swollen-shut eyes seeped watery blood. I unsheathed my knife, cut the ropes that held his arms behind him to a piling, and then rested his head on a cushion I grabbed from the deck. Tom uttered a muffled cry. His bloated lips were too swollen to move. Blood bubbled out and choking sounds came from his throat.

"Quit trying to talk," I said. "We'll get you fixed first. Then we'll find who did this."

I gave my location and described the problem to the 911 operator who told me to stay on the line, but I clicked off my cell and called Billy Fahey, my friend, the Fire Chief, and the paramedics' boss, to give him the identical information.

Billy barked, "Got it, Mick," and the call went dead.

Blood matted Tom's hair, his T-shirt bloody and torn, his

7

chest a mixture of black, blue, and red welts and crusted blood. His arms lay limp by his side and small moans cried out from his unrecognizable face.

"Tom, help is coming," I whispered, and noticed his right ear was half torn from his head.

The first sounds of sirens came quickly. Tom belched blood and made a sound like a word, maybe two, then passed out.

A fire truck pulled into the club's small parking lot. Pat Fraga rushed into the yard first, a large emergency medical bag clutched in his hands. He shook his head in sympathy and disgust and then went to work. Someone tapped my shoulder. Jerry Perkins wanted me out of the way so he could assist.

While Jerry held Tom, Pat poured sterile water over his hair and face, trying to wash away the blood. Jerry put a large four-by-four-inch bandage against Tom's torn ear, but blood continued to seep. He added another one and Jerry used gauze to wrap it in place. Dickie Ward rushed in with a backboard as Pat put a neck brace on Tom. The three men lowered him down onto the board. Somehow, they ignored the sickening moans their actions caused, while the painful sounds echoed in my head.

While they gingerly followed procedure, I found myself repeating the sound Tom had belched at me. The word *gusanos* took shape in my mind, the Cuban government's favorite term for exiles in Miami. It means worm.

A police car and ambulance arrived at the same time. The paramedics came running in, following the directions of the firefighters. The two paramedics and Jerry cut off Tom's shirt; all the time he was crying in pain with soft, bloody moans from his swollen lips. One of the paramedics was setting up an IV bag; I hoped it had morphine in it.

As I moved out of their way—as much to give them room as to escape Tom's cries—I saw Key West Police Officer Danny

Smith. He looked at me, nodded, and turned back toward the paramedics.

"Danny, I think you'd better call the Chief."

"I need to secure this area," he said. "Backup's coming."

A faint drizzle began to fall. The sky darkened, promising a stronger downpour. Even the rain couldn't wash the blood off Tom, as the paramedics worked to move him. Danny walked away, his cell phone stuck to his ear.

"The Chief wants you to call him," Danny said as he walked back. "He asked me what happened and I told him I didn't know yet. Why did someone do that to Tom?" He wiped the dampness from his glasses.

"I don't know, Danny. We were meeting here to hold our Key West-to-Havana sailboat race meeting."

"Tom's a tough guy, I can't see him not putting up a fight, but it doesn't look like he did."

"There's no mess."

I knew from stories told during beers that Tom had done three tours of duty in Vietnam. He didn't look like an ex–machine gunner, lying on the damp ground.

"You guys are close, what do you think it's about?" Danny's glasses steamed over. "The person who did this didn't just want to rob Tom, he wanted to hurt him bad."

"Hell, the only thing on land Tom has worth stealing is his motorcycle, and that's in the parking lot."

One of the paramedics called Danny over and pointed out a two-by-four floating at the shoreline.

"I'm already wet," I said, and walked into the water to retrieve the piece of wood.

As I reached for it, I could see the brown-stained top. I assumed it was Tom's blood. I picked it up carefully and handed it to Danny, who had put on latex gloves.

"Blood?" I asked.

Danny turned it over to the side that had been in the water and stared at the faded stains. "Be my bet," he said, and moved to the deck to find a safe place for the damp piece of wood.

A crowd of curious sailors had gathered outside in the wet parking lot, and the rain became steadier. Jerry cleared the way for the paramedics to roll the gurney with Tom to the ambulance. Within minutes, siren wailing, the ambulance sped down Palm Avenue on its way to the only hospital in Key West.

Danny had the cell phone to his ear and motioned me over. He closed the phone.

"Detective Morales wants you to wait here."

"Damn! Why him?"

"He's the duty officer."

Luis Morales came to the States as a child in a boat from Cuba. He does not have an open mind on the subject of his native country and enjoys reporting boaters that leave Key West for Marina Hemingway to the Coast Guard.

We don't get along.

"Danny, how long before Luis gets here?"

"You can't leave, Mick."

"I know, Danny. I'm wondering how long he's gonna make me wait."

"He's a good cop, I respect him," Danny said.

"He hates me," I said. "Stick around, Danny, I may need a friend."

"I'm here until Morales tells me different."

I sat on a folding chair in the club's tiki-styled clubhouse to get out of the rain, while Danny went to tell the crowd outside there would be no meeting. The sailors began to disperse as the fire trucks drove off. An unmarked city police car, with Morales driving, stopped by the gate.

The rain came down harder, beating on the tin roof of the clubhouse.

Two

Luis Morales, at five-foot-ten, looked more like a Latin model than a Key West detective. His wavy black hair had highlights of gray, his olive complexion, bright smile, and large brown eyes made him handsome and popular with the local ladies. And, he knew it.

Danny Smith stood in the downpour talking to Luis through a half-opened car window. Danny pointed in my direction before walking away to help a newly arrived officer secure yellow crime scene tape across the club's chain-link fence.

Luis stepped out of the car, his KWPD baseball cap pulled down tight and his blue police windbreaker zipped.

I walked to the refrigerator, unlocked it, took out a can of Albertson's ginger ale, and sat back down.

Luis walked slowly from the car, through the gate to the clubhouse deck, as if the rain didn't exist.

"Mick, I am sorry about Tom." He unzipped the windbreaker and took a notepad from his shirt pocket.

"Thanks." I was trying to be polite.

"Officer Smith said you found Tom."

"I did."

"Tell me what you did."

I told him and he wrote. He waited for me to finish before saying anything.

"You cut the ropes holding him to the piling." He pointed to the evidence bag on the deck that held the rope. Luis sat at one of the wooden picnic tables in the clubhouse.

"Yes."

"Did you touch anything else?"

"I got the two-by-four out of the water."

"Do you think that's what they used to beat him?"

"I was hoping you'd tell me."

"CSI will check to see if it's Tom's blood," he said and looked at me. "I wouldn't be surprised."

I didn't answer. He was trying to be polite, too, and I didn't want to say anything that might change that. I took a swallow of ginger ale.

"How many people were to meet you to discuss the race?"

I could feel politeness washing away in the rain, as soon as he mentioned the race. Danny must have put everything I said into his verbal report.

"The usual suspects."

He looked at me again and forced a quick smile. "As many as last year?"

"What difference does it make?"

"In theory, those attending knew where Tom would be this early. I'd like to see if anyone had a grudge. I have to begin somewhere, unless you have an idea."

"I don't think the boaters had anything to do with this," I bit my tongue and didn't say anything about *gusanos*. "I wish I knew who did."

"I wish you did, too, because you would tell me, right?" He wrote something down.

"Of course." He jotted into the notebook and I thought, maybe he was playing a word game with himself.

"Could it have been a robbery?"

"The only things locked at the sail club are the front gate and the refrigerator. There's nothing to steal."

"Could he have found some scumbags sleeping here and it

turned ugly?"

"More likely than thieves."

He scribbled some more and then hesitated, as if he was about to say something. He reread from the notebook, to himself. "What are the chances these perps were looking for you?" His dark eyes turned hard and his thin smile was cold. "Could they have mistaken Tom for you?"

"If they did, they didn't know me," I said. "We don't look anything alike."

"You both have beards and it was early in the morning." He hefted his shoulders and continued to stare at me.

"I have red hair and I always need a haircut," I tried a smile, but it wouldn't come. "Tom's is salt and pepper, they didn't mistake us."

"Anything you're working on that could have you in trouble?"

Being a journalist, I've worked on stories that involved Central American revolutionaries, drug smugglers, politicians and a variety of hoodlums for the weekly news magazines, but this had nothing to do with my career.

"I am not working on anything. The winds are blowing and I want to go sailing."

"To Cuba?"

"Not in these winds, Luis. The Gulf Stream has to have ten- to fifteen-foot waves on average. No one boats over in those conditions."

"Rafters do," he wrote again in the notebook.

Rain pounded the roof, and off to the west I could see lightning and then thunder exploded around us as I silently counted to five. Luis looked up.

"How close was that?" But, he wasn't asking me.

"I hope you find the bastards."

"I'm sure you do." He eyed the crime scene from where we were and continued writing in the notebook.

"Are we finished?" I tossed the empty soda can into the trash barrel.

"For now," he said, without looking up. "The Chief wanted to hear from you."

The weather forced me to leave my dinghy tied at the dock, so I walked the short distance to my live-aboard slip at Garrison Bight Marina. I cupped my cell phone to my ear and called Key West Police Chief Richard Dowley.

"You wanted me to call." I walked along Palm Avenue, rain, thunder, and lightning my companions.

"I was doing yard work when Officer Smith called about Tom," he said, hesitantly. "Tom's in surgery, right now. What are you guys into?"

"Nothing."

"Mick, is he messing with someone's wife? Or are you working on a story and they were looking for you?"

I told him what I had said to Luis about not working on anything at the time. But, I reminded myself that the past had come after me before. Criminals have long memories and survive on revenge, as do Latin drug dealers.

"You think this was random?"

"No."

"You want to come by the house, I'm done with yard work."

"I'm soaked," I said. "It'll be about an hour."

"I'll make us a couple of sandwiches, I'm hungry," and he hung up.

Richard lives in New Town in a two-bedroom blockhouse with his wife, Patty. By the time I arrived, the rain had stopped and the sun was fighting to come out. He greeted me at the door.

The Chief is a big man, six-foot-four, and a good 250 pounds and he has cold brown cop's eyes. Saturday was his day off. Crimes like Tom's beating are rare in Key West. The crime concerned him professionally, but the fact that he knew the victim made it more personal.

"You must be the most punctual guy in Key West," he said, as I walked in. "Sandwiches are in the kitchen."

He had made two ham and cheese sandwiches, dumped a bag of potato chips into a bowl, and poured two mugs of beer. I started right off by telling him everything that had happened from the time I arrived at the sail club.

"Why was Tom there? Why were you there that early?"

"We were having the first meeting for the Key West–Havana race. Tom, Bob Lynds and I were supposed to meet and prepare the place."

"Damn it, Mick, you're gonna bring Treasury back, aren't you?" he said between bites. "Didn't everyone get in enough trouble last year?"

It wasn't a police matter, it was a federal matter, but his officers had to assist the U.S. Custom's officers intercepting the sailboat racers as they returned from Cuba last year. He didn't like losing half his street cops.

"We all have OFAC licenses. We deliver humanitarian aid to Cuba, just like last year."

The federal government had begun hassling boaters going to Cuba a few years ago, and when we arrived back in Key West last year, Customs and Treasury agents from the Office of Foreign Asset Control ignored our licenses. They confiscated cameras, GPSs and anything that could show money had been spent outside Marina Hemingway, or that boaters had traveled while there. As a journalist, I was exempt from the restrictions, but they gave my crew hell. No one had heard anything back since, and it had been a year and the items confiscated had not been returned.

"So is this related?"

"It might be."

It caught him by surprise. He sat up straight in his chair.

"I'm listening."

"Tom only said one word to me, I think."

He waited another long second and shook his head.

"You know, if rubber hoses were still in vogue I'd be using one on you right now." Richard's face muscles tightened.

"He said 'gusanos.'"

"How?" Richard demanded in his cop's voice. "The doctors said his jaw is broken in a couple of places, his nose is busted, he lost teeth and his whole face is swollen. How'd he say *gusanos?*"

"Slowly, but I heard it."

"*Gusanos,* that's Havana slang for the Miami exiles, right?"

"Yeah."

"You and the Miami Cubans aren't exactly friendly, right?"

"What are you getting at, Richard?"

"Mick, I don't need you hearing things that weren't said. It isn't going to help this investigation."

"How long have you known me?"

"I'm a cop right now, Mick, not your friend," he swallowed some beer. "I've got a guy, someone I know, who could be dead before the day's over. He's been beaten savagely and I want to get the people who did it. I don't need to be chasing ghosts. Things like this don't happen in Key West."

We both ate in silence. The crunching of potato chips was the only sound in the house. The beer was cold, but had lost its taste.

"Do you really think this had anything to do with the sailboat race?" he said, to break the silence.

"I don't know. Tom didn't put up a fight, so they caught him by surprise or there had to be a few of them." I sipped my beer. "To the hard-core exiles, this race is like treason. Don't discount what I heard."

"I won't." He got us two cold beers. "Detective Morales has your report, right?"

"He hates us, he's not gonna do a good job."

"He's a damn good detective, and he will do his job. Did you tell him about Tom saying *gusanos?*"

"No, I thought better of it."

"Smart on your part." He smiled for the first time.

"I'm concerned about this, Richard. If this is about the race, it may not be over."

"You're right to be concerned, Mick," he said, and lost the smile.

THREE

A few days later, Bob Lynds called and asked me to meet him at the Tree Bar on the two hundred block of Duval Street. It was early, but he said it was important.

Bob has forgotten more about sailing than I will ever know. He is tall and lean, with long silver hair he keeps in a ponytail, smiling brown eyes and a contagious laugh. When local building contractors get in a pinch, they call him for finish work. He prices his service way above scale. Most of the time, he's working on his classic wooden boat or sailing.

Lu Kim, a young Korean-American with long, silky-black hair, large chestnut eyes, and bronze skin, was behind the empty bar teasing Bob with a smile and feminine laugh, when I walked into the alley.

The Tree Bar sits in an old brick-lined alley shaded by a large gumbo-limbo tree. Premium liquors fill the mirrored shelves and fresh-squeezed citrus juices are used for mixed drinks. A sidewalk away from Duval Street, the bar is a respite from the crowded thoroughfare. The bar, often under attack by vehicle exhaust, loud, obnoxious wanderers, and a tropical sun, was quiet and cool as I took my seat.

Lu works the outdoor bar three afternoons a week and usually tended bar at Rick's next door on the weekends. She tells customers she's North Korean, but forgets to explain the north part comes from Franklin Lakes, N.J., where American parents raised her. Most first-time customers tell her she speaks English well and she thanks them. The tips on the weekends are out-standing.

"Bloody Mary?" Lu said as I sat down.

"Please." I turned to Bob, "What's so important?"

"Lu might have stumbled onto something about who's responsible for Tom." Bob lit a cigar. He offered me one, I took it, and he lit it with a lighter I had given him years ago.

I lose four or five good cigar lighters a year, Bob has had only one since I've know him and it was a gift from me.

Three days had passed since I found Tom beaten at the sail club. He remained in intensive care at the hospital. Morales still hadn't been able to talk to him and Richard had warned me that the medical reports were not good. And, neither was the criminal investigation's progress.

Lu slipped my Bloody Mary in front of me, garnished with a large slice of lime and piece of celery. A beer delivery truck pulled into the loading zone and began taking full beer kegs to Rick's. The dolly clinked and rattled when he returned with empty kegs.

"I didn't think about this until I was talking to Bob last night," Lu's bright eyes were a contrast to her sad expression. "We were talking about Tom and something clicked."

She had been behind the bar at Rick's Saturday night, it was the early hours of Sunday morning, and three Cubans sat drinking shots of rum with beer chasers, celebrating. They were laughing and slapping each other on the back. They hardly noticed the petite Asian bartender and never thought she might be fluent in Spanish.

"One of them asked me what time the Sunday paper came out," she said. "I told him I wasn't sure, and when I asked if he was going to be in it, they laughed and said 'yes,' but wouldn't say what about."

It was busy at two in the morning, so she caught up with

other customers, but kept hearing the loudness of the three men.

"They kept laughing at how surprised this man was, but they always used derogatory words to describe him," she frowned. " 'Son of a whore,' those Cuban macho words, and they kept getting more vulgar as they drank."

"What made you think they were talking about Tom?" I finished my drink.

"Well, they talked a lot about how the guy would never be pretty again, they fixed his face, and when I asked if one of them was going to be citizen of the day in the local daily, they laughed and one said, 'No, we'll make the front page.' "

"And who made Sunday's front page?" Bob blew smoke rings into the air.

"Tom," I said. "Do you know these guys?"

"They've been in before. I think they're from Miami or that neighborhood." Lu wiped the bar with a damp rag, her petite body a beauty in motion. "From what I picked up in their conversations, they boat to Cuba once or twice a month."

"Fishermen?"

"I doubt it, their hands were too soft. They spend a lot of time outdoors, but not doing anything as physical as fishing. Not for a living, anyway."

"Why do you think they meant Tom?" I said again, biting into a lime.

"I make my living by judging people, Mick. I can tell the cheating wives and husbands before the first drink is finished; I know the big tippers and hustlers by their second drink," she stopped in front of me, took my empty glass, and smiled, "and all the phonies as soon as they walk in the door."

"What do you make these guys out to be?"

"Cruel," she said without a smile. "Cowards alone, bullies together."

Bob and I knocked the ash from our cigars and ordered another drink.

"You wanna tell Richard?" Bob rolled his cigar.

"He'd need more than Lu's suspicion to go on." I relit my cigar with Bob's lighter.

"Do we follow it up?"

"From a distance."

"Because they're dangerous?"

"Cruel and dangerous," I said.

FOUR

I rode my bike to Sandy's Café on White Street to meet Bob for *café con leches* on Monday. Sandy's, a small, window-service stand, serves hot *con leches* along with a mixture of breakfast sandwiches and lunches. The *con leche* is a mixture of strong Cuban espresso heaped with sugar and a lot of hot milk, a favorite drink in Key West's Cuban neighborhoods.

The January weather had improved and white clouds sailed across the blue sky and made me want to be out on the water. The sun brightened the street and promised to warm the winter day.

We took our *con leches* to the newspaper vending racks and Bob tossed down a small manila envelope. I opened it and took out computer-generated photos of Lu and two Latin men.

"Those are two of the guys," Bob said.

The men in the photos were smiling, their hands around Lu's thin waist.

"How'd she do this? Where's the third guy?"

"I don't know about the third guy, but she got the shots for Rick's wall-of-shame. She asked them if they wanted to be on it, told them all the regulars were."

"Yeah, but those are all Polaroid's."

"She had the bar back snap quick shots with her digital. The girl has imagination."

Lu keeps her digital camera close because, she said, one day someone famous would come into Rick's and she was going to

22

get that person's photo.

I stared at the photos. They looked like the same shot, and I didn't recognize the two men. Lu had cropped them close and printed two sets on five-by-seven-inch paper.

"Do you recognize them?"

"No."

"Me, either," I said. "Do we take them to Richard?"

Bob hunched his shoulders and drank coffee.

"Maybe we can find out who they really are?" he swirled his Styrofoam cup, to mix the coffee and sugar. "Lu found out their boat's in Conch Harbor and they said it's big and fast."

"Smugglers." I finished my *con leche*. "Could they be smugglers and somehow Tom got mixed up with them?"

"I don't know what Tom would have to do with smugglers, but my guess is that's what they are."

I called Richard and offered to buy him a *con leche* and cheese toast for breakfast and he said he'd be right over.

I put one set of the photos back in the envelope and placed it in my bike's basket. I ordered more *café con leches* for us, along with Cuban cheese toast, and waited for Richard.

He walked down Virginia Street. He was in uniform and nodded to people he passed outside Fausto's market, sometimes stopping to shake hands. Cars sped along White Street and some honked, and he waved at them as he crossed against the light.

"Thank you." Richard sipped his *con leche* as he unwrapped a cheese toast sandwich. "And what's this going to cost me?"

The morning air was already warming, promising sunshine and humidity. It was a chamber of commerce day, and cold blanketed the northeast, making Key West a winter destination of choice. The westerly wind pattern blew warm air from Southern Mexico across Cuba to Key West.

I lay the three photos on top of the wrapped cheese breads.

Richard looked at them and then at me.

"I recognize the bartender," he said between sips and bites. "What else am I looking at?"

"The two guys who have been bragging about beating up Tom." I took a cheese toast, unwrapped it, and dunked it in the *con leche*. "They have a boat at Conch Harbor."

"Who are they bragging to?"

"Lu overhead them last weekend and again when this photo was taken." I took a bite of the toast.

"The bartender?"

"Yeah, the girl in the photo."

"Ah, Lu the bartender. And, you expect me to do what? Arrest them on this information?"

"Roust 'em," Bob said. "See what you can get from them."

"You guys know it doesn't work like that." He chewed on his cheese toast. "Will she come in and talk to Morales? If she does, their attorneys call it bar bragging to impress a cute girl, blame the liquor, and they'll be out."

"Maybe they have warrants out on them?" Bob sipped his coffee. "That would be a reason to bring them in."

"What names did they give her?"

"They're written on the back." I took another bite of my cheese toast.

Richard turned the photos over. "Jose Lopez and Carlos Gonzales. Do you think they're real names?"

"Don't know," I said, "but we can go by the marina and see what names they gave there."

"I don't see a boat name." He looked at the back of the photos again.

"Big and fast." Bob sipped his *con leche*. "We'll find it."

"I'll run the names, but you two stay away from the marina and these two. Deal?"

"Deal," I lied.

FIVE

My forty-foot sloop, *Fenian Bastard,* was on a starboard tack as Bob and I moved her around Fleming Key from Garrison Bight. The wind was light but filled the jib, and we were doing three knots, without the mainsail, through quiet, clear turquoise water. We rolled the jib in and motored around the narrow channel that took us toward Key West Harbor. Just before the Coast Guard base, we dropped anchor, boarded the inflatable dinghy, and motored toward Conch Harbor, a private marina in Key West Bight. The harbor water was choppy and cold and sprayed us as the dinghy cut along.

The city's ferry terminal had a large commuter ship berthed. Conch Harbor, across from the terminal, had two yachts, probably one hundred feet long at its dock. We rode past the marina's channels and slips toward Key West Bight City Marina, and then turned around.

"Lot of sailboats and yachts," Bob said as we made another pass by Conch Harbor.

"Yeah." I turned the dinghy down the first channel.

Most of the marina's slips were full and the names and homeports of the boats appeared on their sterns. We slowed down to eye a couple of boats that shared Miami as home. The water was dark and rainbow-colored gas film floated on sections of it. Some boaters were not careful when topping off fuel tanks and the slimy film floated around the marina for days.

"Big and fast would eliminate the trawlers," Bob said.

In the second channel there was a white go-fast, *Libertad* stenciled on its stern, in one of the slips. I slowed down.

"It's big and looks fast," I said.

"It is. You think Doug's on duty today?"

Doug Bean is the dock master at Conch Harbor and an old sailing buddy. I motored toward the dinghy dock.

"What do you know about go-fasts?"

"They go fast!" Bob laughed.

"Yeah, that's what I thought."

Our world is sailboats and we hadn't learned—or cared to learn—much about motorboats.

"I thought that was you, anchored offshore." Doug walked over to meet us at the dock. "Anything wrong?"

Doug wore his thinning, sun-bleached hair cut short, his sleeveless marina T-shirt was blinding white, while his old cargo shorts were faded from use, and worn flip-flops covered the bottoms of his feet.

We stayed seated in the dinghy and threw a line to him. His baseball cap could not protect him from the tropical sun and his legs, arms, and face were the color of burnt walnuts.

"The go-fast, *Libertad,* how long has it been here?"

"Midweek. Something wrong, Mick?" He gave me a puzzled look.

"Two Cubans come with it?"

"Three." Doug tied the line to a cleat. "They come in once or twice a month."

He looked around and then gave Bob and me a hand up to the dock. As we stood there, he checked the pie r again.

"They in trouble?" We shook hands.

"What makes you think that?"

"Hell, Mick, if they ain't smugglers, no one in this town is."

"Drugs or people?" Bob asked.

"Where's the easy profit these days?"

"People," I said.

Smugglers of Cuban immigrants can get as much as $10,000 per person delivered to American soil. With the federal government's wet-foot/dry-foot policy, Cubans caught on the water are returned to Cuba, while those who reach land are given asylum and a welfare check. There's only a small risk in smuggling human cargo these days, since family members in the States pay the bill and usually arrange the rendezvous location. Once on land, the Cubans want Immigration officers to find them so they can be processed as quickly as possible. There is little chance that "dry" Cubans will be repatriated. Risk, to experienced smugglers, is minimal, though there have been reports of smugglers leaving passengers in the Florida Straits' mangrove islands to perish. Smugglers, when caught and tried, face less than two or three years in jail. Inexperienced smugglers—sometimes family members—have gone out without the proper safety equipment and have perished or, possibly, ended up in Cuban jails.

"It wouldn't surprise me," Doug said. "What's going on?"

We told him how we thought the men were involved in the beating of Tom, but did not mention Lu. Doug identified two of the Cubans from the photos as Jose Lopez and Carlos Gonzales and gave us their Miami marina address. The third man, not in the photos, was Pepe Fernandez. There was little else available since they paid for everything in cash.

I called Richard as we sailed back to Garrison Bight. I told him what we had and he asked me to come to his office, even though it would be dark when I got there. Bob said he didn't feel comfortable in a police station and left me on my own after we docked.

I called from the slip and Richard, in his police blues, was outside the station when I arrived and walked me to his office.

"They used their real names," he said as we walked the empty

27

second-floor corridor. "There are no warrants out for them."

"There's a third one," I said, "Pepe Fernandez."

"I know." We entered his office. "You think these guys are villains." He sat down.

"I know they are." I took a seat in front of his desk.

Richard sat quietly. He turned his back to me and looked out the window. Small dock lights showed at the slips across the street, and headlight glare splashed along North Roosevelt Boulevard below. Stars shimmered in the black sky and the flashing light on the Navy's bachelor officers' quarters building blinked in the distance.

"These guys are well connected in Miami," he turned toward me. "You're right, they're not good guys, but they serve a purpose and you're not going to like it, but I can't touch them."

"You know they did Tom," I was trying to keep my voice controlled, "and you can't touch them?"

"If I had the evidence to arrest them, which I don't, the Feds would come and claim them and that would be that."

"The Feds are protecting them?"

"Kind of, 'my enemy's enemy is my friend,' " he said, but couldn't keep a smile. "I ran the names and within a half hour Feds were calling me. Two agents are coming down to explain things."

I couldn't believe it. Somehow, these men had found a way for the federal government to protect them in their criminal activities, but what had they done to deserve this protection?

"What agency?"

"What's the difference? Up there, it's all one agency. Like a snake with too many heads, it still only has one body."

"And I'm supposed to accept this? I've got outlets that can expose this, it's what I do for a living."

"Yeah, I know," he said, again without a smile, "and I've been told to tell you that if you don't leave it alone your race to

28

Havana will be stopped and everyone in it will lose their boats, or at least they will be tied up in the system for years. Walk away and maybe your race will go on without a problem."

"Sounds like blackmail."

"Not when the government does it. It's called good advice."

"I can't believe this," I said, as I stood. "Aren't you angry?"

"I'm mad as hell, Mick."

"And if Tom dies?"

"I'm glad I don't have to think about that."

"And what about justice?"

"They told me a bigger justice is being served."

"Bullshit!"

Six

Tom died Wednesday, eleven days after the beating. He fought death, but brutality won out. Richard called late that morning with the news.

"Tom never regained consciousness, if it's any consolation," Richard said. "I wanted to tell you personally, but the twit Tommy Foolery from the paper was there, so the word will be out, and I didn't want you hearing it from someone else."

"I appreciate the call," I said.

Tom's condition had gone from bad to worse during the week, and I didn't think he'd make it, but I must have secretly held out some hope because the news left a hollow ache in my chest and I needed to take deep breaths to fill my lungs.

I was at the dock on the *Fenian Bastard,* the sun was out, and a twelve-knot wind was blowing from the southeast. It was a good day to be sailing, and I thought how awful for a sailor to die on a day like this. The wind carried the salt scents off the Gulf Stream and the bright sky looked like the reflection of the gulf itself.

"It's murder now," I said.

"Yes, I know. I need to contact Tom's family."

He was changing the subject from murder and I let him, because if I spoke my mind it might've been the beginning to the end of our friendship, and losing another friend was something I didn't need.

"He fought in Vietnam and was a damn good sailor. He probably has some contact info on his boat. Most of us leave a note on who to contact . . . just in case."

"Tell me where the boat is and I'll meet you there."

"Peninsular Marina on Stock Island," I said. "Richard, what do you do now?"

"We'll talk about that at the marina. Half an hour?" He avoided answering my question.

"I'm leaving now." I hung up.

North Roosevelt Boulevard runs past Garrison Bight Marina. The four-lane road is constantly busy with traffic heading to and from Old Town, and off the island. Tom always revved his motorcycle's engine extra loud as he passed my slip, his way of saying hi. I walked along the floating dock to the parking lot and realized he wouldn't be doing that anymore. How long would it take me not to look up when I heard a motorcycle's engine rev on the boulevard?

It was a slow ride, on a beautiful day, to Peninsular Marina.

I found a phone number for Tom's sister taped to the bottom lid of his chart table and gave it to Richard. All his boat insurance and military papers were in large envelopes in the aft cabin.

"I'll see she gets everything," he said as we stood in the main cabin. "Does she know you?"

"I don't know her."

If the cabin's walls could talk, they would have been loud with laughter and sea stories of men and women who had spent time aboard enjoying life. How many times had Bob and I helped Tom with some dirty, sweaty project on this boat and how many times had he helped us with problems on our boats? Though each project had been work, it resulted in beers, cigars and, most importantly, laughs.

I left reluctantly because I would never be back. I looked around the cabin one last time, missing Tom.

Outside Richard closed the hatch and looked for a lock.

31

"Most live aboard don't lock 'em," I said to his puzzled look.

Low-flying Navy jets screamed across the sky. Boca Chica Navy Base was opposite the bay and when pilots were in the Keys for flight training the sky thundered and the ground shook.

"Where are you going?" Richard said as I got into my old Jeep.

"I can use a drink. You?"

"I want to take care of this." He raised the large envelope with all of Tom's information.

"It's a murder investigation now, right?" I said between the thundering jets landing and taking off.

"A police murder investigation, when we come up with something, I'll let you know, Mick."

Richard climbed into his unmarked patrol car and rolled down the window.

"I want to solve this. I want to get whoever did this as much as you do." He had a hurt look, as though he knew I didn't believe him.

I nodded and drove off wondering how he would handle the murder investigation and the Feds.

Parking in Old Town is difficult at best, even on weekdays. I pulled into B.O.'s Fish Wagon's parking lot. Buddy Owens owns the fish shack, but his truck wasn't there so I walked toward Schooner Wharf Bar.

Schooner has been around for about twenty years. The bar looks out at a harbor that has two private marinas filled with million-dollar yachts. Shrimp boats filled the harbor twenty years ago and white-booted shrimpers occupied the bar's stools then. Schooner has four floating docks of its own filled with classic wooden boats, attached to the pier. The bar is nothing more than some thatched roofing and gnarled driftwood planking. Old, uncomfortable wooden bar stools sit along the bar's railing. There are no doors or windows, it is open to the elements, and its weathered and beaten look is well deserved. A covered stage fills one side of the pebbled courtyard and there is entertainment from noon to midnight, seven days a week, rain, or shine. Small, brightly painted tables fill the courtyard, some with umbrellas; larger tables have their own thatched roofs. A small fry-kitchen fronts the restrooms and serves a great fish sandwich.

A humid breeze blew in off the water as I took a seat at the bar. The sky was ocean blue and wisps of white clouds skipped across it. The salty smell off the Gulf mixed lazily with the aroma of cigar and cigarette smoke, stale beer and songs about Key West that flowed from singer Michael McCloud's stage speakers. Noisy conversations competed with the music.

I don't know where my mind was. I was angry and sad, but I couldn't focus on my feelings or what to do about them. I wanted to get drunk, real drunk, but feared the dreams that would arise from the depths of my subconscious; the same dreams I tried to drown with alcohol until I decided alcohol might have been the cause of them.

I accepted a Kalick, a Bahamian beer, from the bartender and took the steps up to a small room that had a large-screen TV and one pool table. The TV was on, but the sound was off and I was by myself. I sat down, looked out at the boats, and wondered why they were in slips and not out enjoying the water. Why wasn't I on the water? I wondered, pushed the slice of lime down the bottle's long neck, and drained my beer.

"How's that for timing?" Padre Thomas Collins placed a Kalick on the table and sat down.

Thomas is one of many idiosyncratic characters that find refuge in Key West. He's a Jesuit missionary priest, in his late fifties, who one day walked away from the mission rectory because the angels told him to. He sees and communicates with

33

angels and sometimes the wisdom he surprises me with makes me believe him. He's a little taller than six feet, very thin—soaking wet he couldn't weigh one hundred and fifty pounds—and has the palest blue eyes I've ever seen. His skin is sunburned a brownish red from spending so many hours outdoors. Home is a small efficiency apartment on William Street and he gets around the island on a bicycle or by foot.

He wore a collarless, washed-out yellow shirt with the sleeves torn off, cutoff jeans without a belt and sandals, his regular attire. Two packs of Camel cigarettes, one opened, were in his shirt pocket.

Thomas still considers himself a priest, and I have seen him talking with the pastor of St. Mary Star of Sea, the local Catholic Church, but I have never heard of him saying Mass. Rumor is that the Church pays him a stipend to stay away, but rumors run rampant over the small island and are very rarely true.

"Thank you," I said, taking the beer as Thomas sat down. "How are you Padre?"

"How are you, Mick?" His pale eyes probed me.

Sometimes, when talking with Thomas, I have the feeling his eyes are searching for my soul. He could be laughing, but if you glanced into his eyes, the intensity was scary.

"Any better, I'd be illegal." I smiled and took a swallow of the beer he'd brought.

He sipped from his Budweiser. He looked outside and watched tourists stop and stare at the tall ships berthed there. One of the boat's mates took a photo of a family as they stood in front of the Schooner *Western Union*.

A soft breeze came in the open windows and helped the room's slow-swirling ceiling fan do its job.

"I was sorry to hear about Tom," he said, never taking his stare away. "I've prayed for him."

"Thank you," was all I could say.

Thomas took out an unfiltered Camel cigarette and lit it. He inhaled deeply.

"You don't want to talk about it?" He stubbed out the Camel.

"About what?"

"About Tom. It had to be horrible finding your friend beaten like that."

"Is this confession, Padre?"

"Why?" he grinned. "Have you already been?"

"Yeah," I said, "with Father Chief of Police."

"Mick, don't misjudge your friends." He lit another Camel. "You're better than that and know things are never as simple as they appear. Richard is a good cop."

"Yeah, but will he go up against the Feds?"

"He'll do what's right." He sipped some beer. "What will you do?"

"I haven't thought that far yet."

"Tom is at peace now." His eyes like rivets. "No one can hurt him any longer. You need to find peace, Mick."

"I can't let his death go unpunished," I said through clenched teeth.

"I think you have more to make peace with than that. Since I've met you, you have been at war with yourself." He blew smoke over my shoulder. "You have probably fooled everyone but yourself and me. Make peace with yourself, Mick, and dealing with Tom's death will be easier. Maybe you'll even see the world as a better place."

Since first meeting Padre Thomas sitting on a bar stool eight years ago at Schooner, he has seemed to know about my darkest secrets. Of course, I've told myself, he couldn't. I escaped to Key West, but not from myself and the horrible truths of my past I have difficulty living with.

Ten years I've been gone from Los Angeles, taking eighteen months to sail to Key West. Eighteen months, eight-and-a-half years later and my nightmares are no less real than the afternoon the bomb blew up the car in Tijuana, Mexico. The bomb I'd put in a briefcase. It was covered with money, money that bought the release of a friend who had come there to help me swindle a Mexican drug kingpin. It was supposed to kill him, a man who had escaped justice because of corruption in high places in too many countries.

Almost every night since, I've dreamed the same dream. Dick Sullivan gets out of the car—its windows are tinted—a man with a gun is leading him. Sully stops, but the man continues to me. I open the briefcase, show him the money, and close it. I hand over the case—it's set to explode on the second opening—and as the man walks away Sully rushes to me. He is trying to tell me something, but I can't make it out. Cars are circling the rotary sections of Avenida de los Heroes. I can hear the noise and smell the exhaust, even though it's a dream.

"Mel's in the car," Sully yells twenty feet away from me.

The man hands the case through the car's back window, gets in and begins to drive away.

"Mel's in the car!" Sully yells again.

As his words are understood, I see the car move and then explode. Sully turns when the explosion goes off, a look of horror on his face as he runs to me. Alfonso Ruiz, my Mexican friend, grabs me and pulls me to his waiting car. I can't stop looking at the car as it smokes and burns. Sometimes in the dream, I can see Mel sitting in the car and watch her burn up.

We had been close for years. I loved her, and I can only speculate on what our future would have been, but that's a waste of time. She was there to help us sting the drug lord with a money-laundering scheme. I killed her because I allowed her to get involved, and I killed her with a bomb I handed over.

Knowing it was an accident, something Sully, Alfonso, and other friends involved in the scheme kept telling me, did not release me from what I felt was my responsibility. I have so much to be angry with myself for and, though I know Padre Thomas is right, I am unable to let it go.

"Time, Padre," I said, "it heals all wounds, right?"

"If we let it. Sometimes we need help to get time to work for us."

He lit another Camel and my hand went to my pocket for a cigar, but it was empty, so I took a long hit on the Kalick.

"You know, Mick, angels are warriors," Thomas said while exhaling smoke.

"What?" I wasn't sure where the statement had come from.

"Angels, you know, today's TV shows about angels helping people, they aren't too off track," he grinned and his eyes brightened. "But angels are God's warriors and sometimes turning the other cheek just isn't the right way to go."

"I thought Jesus taught turning the other cheek."

"Yes, he did, but Jesus is the son and God is the father." He stubbed out the Camel. "Sometimes God's work has to be done by warriors."

"You've lost me, Padre. Are we talking about the Old Testament?"

"I've heard you may have a lead on who killed Tom." He ignored my Biblical comment and finished his beer. "Want another one?"

He got up without waiting for my answer and walked to the bar.

Key West is a small island, and anyone trying to keep a secret is going to get a quick lesson in futility. The often called "coconut telegraph" spreads news—real and imaginary—around the island faster than a local lobster escaping a diver.

Thomas often used angels when explaining his actions or opinions, and I had a feeling I was in for one of his angel explanations and a cold beer when he returned.

SEVEN

"I ordered two fish sandwiches." Thomas put a cold beer in front of me. "You look hungry."

By ordering food, Thomas didn't have to pay for the beers, and he probably didn't pay for the first two, either, because the waitress would put it all on one bill. A bill that would come to me after Thomas left. It wasn't the first time I'd allowed him to get beer, it wouldn't be the last, and it never bothered me.

He lit a Camel and pulled a cigar from his shirt pocket.

"You need this more than a beer," he laughed and lit a match for me.

He was right. A cigar seemed to relax me more than a drink. Sailing the Florida Straits to Cuba can be a twelve- to fourteen-hour trip without liquor, but it always required a few good cigars.

"Thank you." I leaned into the match and lit the cigar. The Cuban roller that sells cigars at Schooner has a good five-dollar cigar.

"Is it true?" he said as I blew out the first thick smoke.

"Is what true?"

"That you have an idea who killed Tom."

"Maybe."

" 'Maybe' because you don't want to talk about it, or 'maybe' because you're not sure?"

"Not sure," I said enjoying the cigar. "What are you getting at, Padre?"

The waitress delivered our two fish sandwiches. Three large pieces of dolphin—called mahi-mahi on the menu so the tourists wouldn't think they were eating Flipper—surrounded with fries.

"I'm just thinking out loud what others are talking about."

Bob had told me a couple of days before that people along the waterfront had already heard we had checked out some Cubans, but that was all they had. Lu's name was never mentioned, and it would've been if the people spreading the rumors had a clue about her. Of course, by now the rumors probably had us feeding the Cubans to the sharks and another Key West legend would be born. Maybe Michael McCloud would write a song about it in a year or two, and Jimmy Buffett would have another hit.

"What are you hearing, Padre?"

"Trash from the locals." He bit into the sandwich.

He doused his fries in ketchup. I put hot sauce on the fish and fries, added salt and ketchup.

"But?" I joined him in eating.

"You know I have more reliable sources," he said between bites.

"The angels?"

"Yeah," he grinned, "sometimes, Mick, I honestly think you believe me."

"Sometimes I do, Padre, sometimes I do."

We finished our sandwiches without talking. My cigar went out, I relit it and drank the last of my beer. The waitress walked through to check on us and I ordered two more beers as she took the empty plates.

"Sometimes is more than most people." He lit a Camel. "If I told you that you were on the right scent, would it mean anything to you?"

I sat back in the seat and puffed on the cigar. He never looked away as he waited for my answer.

"I'm not a hound dog, Padre. I don't hunt."

"You're looking for Tom's killers. Isn't that a hunt?"

"That is what the rumors say, but I've been working on my boat the last few days. I haven't even been fishing."

He sipped his beer and appeared a little nervous as he put the cigarette out. He looked into the bar and then out at the docks. Was he looking for his angels? I smiled with the thought, and it was probably the first time I'd smiled in the past ten days.

"The three Cubans you think did this, did it," he said. He leaned closer to me. "They are bad people and will get away with it if you don't do something."

I was startled as I listened to him.

"How do you know this?" I bit down on the cigar. "Who is telling you these stories?"

Bob, Lu, Richard, Doug, and I are the only people to have any inkling on this and I doubt any of them talked to Padre Thomas, or anyone else.

"Maybe it was your guardian angel, maybe Tom's."

"I'd like to talk with Tom's guardian angel."

"Because Tom died?"

"Because he was murdered," I said. "Some guardian angel."

Thomas sighed and drank his beer. "You have to have faith, Mick."

"In angels and a God that would let someone like Tom die the way he did?"

"Yes." His pale blue eyes bore down on me.

"Why?"

He laughed. "Once, an old Irish priest, Bishop Breslin, if my memory serves me, heard my confession and I told him I had my doubts about my calling because I couldn't understand how God allowed horrible things to happen in the world. Why, I wanted to know, didn't He stop them? You know what he told me?"

"God works in mysterious ways."

"Yeah, that's what I was expecting." He lit another Camel. "Let me explain it in a way you might understand. Your first bike had training wheels, right?"

"Yeah."

"Your father took the training wheels off one day, probably a summer afternoon, and held the bike and ran along as you pedaled, right?"

"How do you know this?"

"You're middle-class Boston, Mick, you all had first bikes and fathers and summer afternoons. He ran along with you, right?"

"Yeah."

"And at some point you looked and saw he'd let go and you were on your own."

"OK."

"Did you ever fall and scrape your knees or hands?"

"A few times," I laughed, and could almost see my father next to me.

"Was that your father's fault?"

"Of course not, I was just learning."

"How many times did you fall or have accidents after you were a good rider?"

"Enough."

"Your father's fault?"

"There's a point to this, right?"

"Oh yeah." He stubbed out the cigarette. "You see, your father could help you learn to ride the bike, but he had to let you go on your own and hope you would be okay. That's what God has done, Mick. He has given us what we need, and it is time for Him to let go. He's no more responsible for Tom's

41

death than your father's responsible for your bike accidents, but your father gave you the bike, and God has given us free will. And we are responsible for how we use it."

Our fresh beers came and we both took long swallows.

I had never heard God explained so simply. The Church was missing a good priest.

"So the responsibility of Tom's death . . ."

"Is on the three Cubans," he said before I finished. "They are evil men and if they aren't stopped they will kill again."

"And I am supposed to do what?"

"Bring them to justice."

"How? Did the angels offer any suggestions?"

"Now you sound like a nonbeliever." He sat back in his chair.

"It's been a long time since I've ridden a bike, Padre."

"I ride one every day. In this town it helps me remember to pray."

I told him what Richard had said about the Feds protecting the three men.

"First, you must try with Richard. The Chief's a good man, he'll do what he can."

"And if he can't do anything?"

"Then you have to find a way to bring them to justice."

"It ain't that easy, Padre."

"The angels didn't say it was easy, Mick."

"I'd like, just for once, to talk to these angels."

"You can always talk to them, Mick, it's called prayer, but it doesn't have to sound like one, and you don't need to be on your knees in church."

"No, I'd like to talk to them face-to-face. It'd make this whole justice thing a lot easier."

"I know you're being sarcastic, Mick, but I don't know why I can see and talk to them and you can't." He sipped his beer. "I didn't believe it at first. I thought I'd lost my mind, like I was turning into one of those religious zealots who claim God talks to them. But, the angels never really ask me to do anything. They just helped me sort through questions on my calling and have stayed with me."

I didn't know what to think. He spoke clearly, but softly. He must have given good sermons from the pulpit once. His voice was firm, and I knew he believed everything he was saying. But, did I? Was he crazy or gifted? And, where did I fit in those categories?

"The Irish priest that heard your confession told you the story about the bike?" I asked, because I didn't have anything else to say.

"Something similar from my childhood, but I understood the meaning."

EIGHT

Padre Thomas left after telling me the bicycle anecdote; he rode his bike to the soup kitchen where he volunteered as cook, server, dishwasher, and counselor. The waitress brought the bill and I paid for the beers, lunch, and cigar. No big surprise.

I sat back in the chair and slowly sipped the last of the Kalick and enjoyed what remained of the cigar. Tourists strolled along the waterfront, stopping to stare at the classic schooners and swift-moving tarpon as they splashed through the blue water. Winter in the tropics, another perfect day in paradise, with a soft breeze and sunshine, and the concept of violent death was nowhere; people came to Key West to celebrate life and leave behind—for a while—the commonplace existence of home. Those of us who had successfully escaped to the island paradise, and called it home, were no different.

Thomas and his angels had forced me to face something I had been avoiding; something I knew would eventually come about even if Tom had lived. I needed to find out who did this and why. Was someone from my past coming after me and, by some crazy ill fortune, mistaken Tom for me? Could Tom have been fooling around with someone's wife? Or was there a reason eluding me?

"*Gusanos,*" he mumbled with the last of his strength as I held him. Three small syllables that took in a lot of territory, but I knew it meant Miami Cubans. What did they want with Tom or me? And, I knew Bob fit into the equation. He could have arrived first at the sail club. Was killing someone to stop the Key West–Havana race logical? All anyone had to do was read the headlines in the *Sun-Sentinel* or the *Miami Herald* to discover how violent some of the old anti-Communist Cubans can be, even with Fidel out of the picture. Their belief was that the end result justified their actions and the death of one sailor would mean nothing to them.

Assuming Tom knew what he was saying, I had one clue, and that led to Lu's overhearing three Cubans, drunk on rum and beer chasers, hinting at something sinister that would show up in Sunday's paper. On the other hand, as Richard said, were they just showboating for a pretty face? How related were the clues? And then the names of two macho Cubans led to federal agents showing an interest in Chief Dowley's search into the Cubans' identities. Coincidence?

I have spent most of my adult life writing investigative pieces for magazines and newspapers, but I had never been personally involved in what I investigated. Normally, a newspaper or news magazine would contact me about a feature they were interested in and I would be off. It was usually to Central America because I had a history there and knew many of the players. It seemed, I thought as I crushed out the cigar and left Schooner Wharf, that not being part of the story was going to change.

I called Bob's cell phone as I headed back to the marina. He didn't answer, so I left a message for him to call me.

Back on the *Fenian Bastard*, I found my Glock 29, a subcompact version of the full-size model 20. I took it from its oily rag wrappings, stripped it down, and cleaned it. I unloaded all four, fifteen-round clips and reloaded them. I realized halfway through the exercise that my hands were shaking as I picked up the bullets and began reloading the clips. I held a half-full clip in the palm of my hand and squeezed it, feeling its coolness, and ran my thumb across the oval tip of the bullet.

I had spent so many years trying not to think about the violence in my past and then, in only a few minutes, the fear I feared slowly emerged. And, in a strange way, it gave me a feeling of contentment, or purpose, and I finished loading the clips with steady hands. I loaded one fifteen-round clip into the Glock. It felt strange, but it was not uncomfortable. I snapped on the clipdraw piece to the body of the Glock, it replaced the need for a holster, and I slipped it on to the back of my old cargo shorts.

When was the last time I had worn this, I wondered as I stood up. The fact smashed me head-on as I remembered Tijuana. The Glock pulled on my shorts from the back, and I realized I would need to start wearing a belt and some old Tommy Bahama shirts to hide it. I took the gun off and put it on the chart table. Why had I kept it? I didn't know. Maybe because it was a gift from my friend Norm? Norm, who stood for everything I was against, but somehow we had been friends.

I have never been sure what government agency he worked for, but I knew he was an operative and spent a lot of time in Central America and the Caribbean in the '80's. He trained professional boxers, had a stable of Latin fighters, and that was his cover.

He was a great background source for many pieces I'd written in the '80s and early '90's, and when push came to shove, he'd defended me as a friend against some malicious people. Against my wishes, he'd gotten me out of Mexico and back to Redondo Beach, California, after Mel's death in Tijuana. He was cruel and tough and that helped me live and finally find the resolve to leave California. Norm had sailed with me as far as the Caribbean side of Panama and then he left me on my own.

I called him once from Key West, maybe seven years ago, now, and he called me back once—I don't remember when—from Miami where he had a boxer fighting. He had his job and

I had my life back, so we moved in different directions.

As I rewrapped the Glock and clips in the oily rag—to keep the moisture away—Bob called. I left everything wrapped on the chart table.

"Clint Bullard's playing at the Hog," he said. "Meet you there?"

"Around six," I answered. "We gotta talk."

"Is everything okay?"

"Maybe. Just be careful, Bob," I said. "I talked with Padre Thomas this afternoon."

"Did you see any angels?" he laughed and hung up.

The downside of winter in Key West is that it gets dark early. The boat slips' electrical outlet boxes splashed soft light along the floating dock as I stepped off the boat. The sky was dark, spotted with stars and an almost full moon. The breeze was cooler than earlier, but I still wore my cargo shorts and T-shirt. Because the Glock was out of its hiding place, I locked the boat and headed toward my Jeep.

Traffic hummed along North Roosevelt Boulevard, packs of scooters zipped around, beeping their tinny horns in unison—a tourist ritual locals couldn't understand.

I was halfway up the parking lot ramp before I saw the man standing in the shadows of the mangroves, smoking. People at the marina, especially the live aboards, are friendly and dress casually, but this guy was overdressed for the water. He wore dress shoes, slacks, and a white shirt. He was six-foot, and his long curly hair was thin on top, stringy on the sides and back. A newly sprouted goatee covered his chin. He tossed the cigarette into the water as I approached.

"*Vivas aquí?*" he asked in Spanish.

"*Sí,*" I answered, and as I got closer, he looked familiar. "I live here. You lookin' for someone?"

"No," he smiled. "I want my boat here tomorrow. For a few

days . . . are good slips now?" he asked in broken English.

"This is a live-aboard dock," I told him, stopping. "There's a waiting list to get a slip."

"Oh," he mumbled, "I need for a few days . . . another dock?"

"Transient slips, that's what you want."

"*Tú vives aquí?*" he asked and pointed down the dock while he lit another cigarette.

"*Sí,*" I said, and with the brief light from the match, I thought he looked a lot like one of the Cuban's in Lu's photos. Why did he care where I lived? I turned suddenly, checking to see if anyone was behind me. The parking lot was well lit and other boaters moved between cars and docks, but weren't paying attention to us.

"*Hermoso . . . es tuyo?*"

"My boat is at the very end," I lied.

"*Grande!* What is it?" he asked and stared down the shadowy pier.

"It's a yawl," I said.

"*No se barco de vela,*" he admitted. "*Gracias.*"

He walked to a Lincoln Town Car, got in the passenger side, and it drove off. I was spooked.

NINE

The knots in my stomach tightened as I drove out of the marina's parking lot on my way to the Hog's Breath Saloon. It wasn't much past six, but it was dark, and each time I stared into the rearview mirror I laughed nervously at myself because I couldn't tell if anyone was following me or not on the busy street. Habit, I guess, kept me glancing at the mirrors; old surveillance habits that I thought were long forgotten. I was on Palm Avenue, a two-lane road, and a line of traffic tailed behind, churning my gut. Twice, at red lights, I fought the desire to go back and get the Glock.

By the time I found a parking spot, I'd convinced myself that the man at the marina had been one of the Cubans in Lu's photo. That, I kept repeating to myself, was not a good sign.

The Hog's Breath is off Duval Street at the Gulf end of the island. Its two outdoor bars were in an open patio with a canopy-covered stage to protect entertainers and their equipment from the tropical elements. The bar's uneven, cracked-cement floor flooded in areas whenever it rained. The larger bar served mixed drinks and bottled beers, the smaller one served draft beer, oysters, shrimp, and other varieties of raw shellfish. The small, wood-platform stage could hold four if the band squeezed in and put the drummer in the back, and had two large speakers and a sound-system control unit set on top of the railing. Mounted fans, with a misting system, helped cool the patio in the summer.

A large, old sea grape tree grew into the stage and its bulky branches extended over the patio and out into the parking lot. Free-range chickens and roosters roamed the parking lot and often climbed the tree to roost. Sometimes patrons were privy to an unofficial cockfight as two or more colorful roosters fought over a hen. It had to be a topic about life in Key West when they arrived home.

Another old tree grew farther down outside the big bar, but leaned inward and had branches overhanging the bar's roof. The city's tree commission would not allow the bar to remove the trees, and to trim the tree back you needed the commission's permission.

Clint Bullard, barefoot and in shorts, was singing "The Best Thing About Her," an original song of his as I walked in. Bob was standing off to the backside of the stage talking to Burt Carroll, another one of our sailing and drinking buddies. I pushed my way between patrons standing around the front of the stage and the raw bar and made it to Bob as Clint finished his song. He yelled hi and I waved as I finally made it to the back of the stage.

"Bobby!" I yelled to the young Irish bartender, leaning under the mounted TV that faced the other side of the bar.

"Comin', Mick!" he yelled back.

Bobby handed me a plastic cup filled with Jameson's and ice. Everything was served in plastic along Duval Street. I took a sip and toasted Bob and Burt. It was too loud to talk—well, a person could talk all they wanted, it was just too loud to hear what was being said without yelling.

Clint was singing "Say Hello to My Heart," another original song, and the crowd was singing along. He played regularly at the Hog—two-week gigs and then back in six weeks—and was popular with the local crowd. A Texas-born singer-songwriter, he now lived and wrote in Nashville.

"You sounded concerned on the phone," Bob said, as Clint asked the patrons what they wanted to hear next.

"I'm more concerned now." I told them about the Cuban at the dock before I left and how I was pretty sure he was one of the men in the photos Lu had given us.

"How sure are you?" Bob asked, as Clint began a song Jerry Jeff Walker recorded—"Desperadoes Waiting for the Train."

"Sure enough and concerned enough that I'll be carrying next time I leave the boat," I told them. "You or I could've gotten to the sail club before Tom."

"I've thought about that way too much," he admitted. "So, what do we do? Keep lookin' over our shoulders?" He drained what beer was left in his Dos Eques bottle.

"How'd Padre Thomas know about any of this?" I asked him. "You, me, Doug and Richard . . ."

"And Lu," he reminded me. "But I don't know who would've talked to the crazy priest."

Bob, a native Oklahoman, didn't have much good to say about a radical Catholic Priest, especially one he thought was defrocked. He claimed the talk about angels was a scam Padre Thomas used to get free drinks.

Bob pulled Burt aside as Clint began another Texas songwriter's song—"The Road Goes on Forever"—and brought him up-to-date on what we were talking about. Most patrons in the crowded bar sang along, making it even more difficult to talk.

Burt is lanky, with ash-blonde hair and a bushy mustache, and needs glasses to see anything farther than his nose. He is a saltwater sailor who delivers expensive sailboats for builders and owners anywhere along the East Coast to the Caribbean and Gulf of Mexico. Bob and I signed on as crew once to help him bring a forty-six-foot Amel Maramu from the Yucatan to Fort Lauderdale. Of course, we made a stop in Havana on our way to Florida.

"I don't have any charters lined up," Burt said after listening to Bob, and Clint had finished the song. "Count me in on whatever you're planning. I liked Tom."

Burt had been on a charter delivery for the past month, and had found out about Tom when he came back to town a few days before our meeting.

It was a little after seven when Clint took a break and we ordered another round.

"So you think the Cubans are still here," Bob said.

"Why wouldn't they be?" I sipped my whiskey. "Doug said they come to the marina a lot."

"And if they've found where you live, it's for a reason," Burt said.

"Yeah." I took a long swallow of Jameson's. "I mean, I just . . ." I couldn't finish my thought. I took another drink. "All this over the sailboat race?"

"Doesn't make sense," Burt agreed.

"Could make sense to the Miami Cubans." Bob toyed with his beer bottle. "Maybe they wanted to set an example and got carried away."

When Clint came back to the stage we moved toward the Front Street entrance of the bar to escape being so close to the speakers.

"You guys were like the 'The Three Stooges,' " Burt said, referring to Bob, Tom, and me. "So if this is about the race, they know all of you. Chances are they don't know me, since I've been gone for a month."

"Your point?" I chewed on a piece of ice from my drink.

"Let me hang around the dock tomorrow, talk to Doug and see what's happening," he suggested. "I have the scooter and I can zip around and follow them without being too noticeable. It's a small island, you keep running into the same people at bars and restaurants and on the street."

"And then what?" Bob asked.

"I've got to find out what happened," I admitted and took a fresh drink from Irish Bobby. "But I don't want to put you guys in jeopardy."

"Hell, Mick, I ain't doing this for you," Burt said. "I'm doing it for Tom."

"There's something else that's possible." I finished my second drink. "This could have nothing to do with the race."

Bob and Burt stood quietly and stared, waiting for me to finish.

"It could be someone from my past. I've done stories on some bad hombres and it could be payback time," I admitted. "It could be all about me."

No one said anything and I could hear Clint finishing "What Turns You On."

"If it's all about you, they still killed Tom, and that's where they made a mistake," Bob said. "If they're stupid enough to mistake Tom for you, they gotta be off the wall and I wanna get 'em. I don't, at this point, care what their reasons were."

"To vengeance," Burt toasted with his plastic cup of scotch, "and it's sweet taste," he added, and drained his drink. "Isn't it time we got a cigar and went somewhere quiet to discuss this?"

On Front Street we mixed with the tourists and headed toward the Key West Sunset Cigar Company, a block away.

"What's the chance you're on the wrong track with these Cubans?" Burt asked outside the cigar store.

"Oh, none," Bob answered sarcastically. "The angels have assured Mick, right?"

Burt looked and smiled. "Ah, the priest?"

"That's what he told me this afternoon."

"Damn, I knew he wasn't crazy," Burt laughed and walked into the cigar shop.

TEN

"I don't like you getting involved," I told Bob and Burt as our evening continued. We sat enjoying our cigars at the Tree Bar, watching the nightly circus of tourists parade along Duval Street; a mass of people, most holding drinks in plastic cups, wandered the street with the force of the Gulf Stream.

At home they might have been salesmen, housewives, schoolteachers, even corporate executives, but in Key West they were adventurers, buccaneers and fools, who celebrated along the busy street with unnamed conspirators for a few hours and consumed their weight in alcohol, like it was a carnival.

The night air was cool, but in most cases, it was warmer than where they came from, so it was something to celebrate.

Bob and Burt had been my friends since I sailed into Key West Harbor, but neither had ever experienced anything in life like the treachery that took Tom's life. I'd follow either man to sea and face the elements of nature with them, but I couldn't ask them to get involved in something their wildest imaginations couldn't grasp.

Live music bombarded the street corners from four bars: Sloppy Joe's, Irish Kevin's, the Lazy Gecko, and Rick's.

We smoked our cigars, sipped our drinks and schemed quietly, covered by the rowdiness of Duval Street. The parade of people went in both directions.

"How can it hurt to see what they're up to?" Burt asked again.

I couldn't explain the ways being caught by these Cubans could hurt. If I told them the truth I'd learned through my experiences they would not—they could not—believe me. Neither had been to war and witnessed or participated in violent death, and the more I tried to persuade them to leave it alone, the more they insisted. I didn't need baggage as I looked into who killed Tom, and I didn't need another friend to die.

"Whatever we're gonna do, let's coordinate it," I said, to placate them, and hoped I could keep them at a safe distance. "Let's not do anything alone."

"Are we looking for anything specific?" Burt asked.

"Let's just find out if they're still on the island." Doug, I knew, could tell us that, but it seemed like the least dangerous thing for Burt to do.

"I'll check in with Doug in the morning," Burt said. "Should I keep tabs on them if they're still here?"

"Hang out with Doug a little while, keep your eyes open and then we'll meet for lunch," I enjoyed my cigar. "Just don't go off on your own."

My cell phone vibrated. It was almost ten. I looked at the screen and saw it was Richard Dowley calling, and answered.

"Yeah, Chief."

"Can you come by the station?"

"In the morning?"

"Now," he said. "Right now."

"Is something wrong?"

"Yes or no, Mick. I wouldn't be asking if I didn't need to see you. And, Mick, come by yourself."

"Yeah," I said, and he hung up. "That was Richard, he wants me to come by the station right now."

"Maybe he has some news on Tom's murder?" Bob guessed.

"He didn't sound all that excited," I lied. "I'll see you at

B.O.'s for lunch."

Richard was waiting for me outside by the fountain. He was in
dark dress slacks and shirt and didn't smile or offer to shake
hands. When I got near the fountain, he turned and walked to
the main door. He punched in the code and the door unlocked.
I followed him into the lobby, but instead of turning at the
stairs to his office, he walked down the hallway. We stopped
outside the police gym.

"Mick, there are two Feds here to see you, off the record."
Richard stood by the gym's glass door. "Whatever good you
think I can be to you, I have already been. These are serious
guys and it seems you're a pain in their ass."

"Should I have a lawyer?" I smiled, but Richard wasn't smiling back. "Richard, I've dealt with Fed hard-asses before. I
haven't done anything, so what do they want with me?"

"It has to do with the three Cubans." He opened the door.

The new gym equipment was still shiny. Barbells and free
weights filled one section of the room and Nautilus equipment
took up the rest of the space. Two men in suits stood off center
and waved us forward, the mirrored walls multiplying their images.

Both were more than six-foot tall, and looked in good shape,
if you could judge with them wearing expensive suits. One was
Latino and had a dark goatee sprinkled with gray. The other
was an Anglo with a military haircut, and he wore glasses.

"Mr. Murphy," the Latino nodded. "Chief, thank you. We
can handle it from here."

"Hold on, Cisco," I said purposely to be rude. "If the Chief
goes, I walk. There are two of you and I have no idea who you
are."

"We are federal agents, Chief Dowley explained that, didn't
he?" the Latino asked.

"Yeah," I smiled, "but I haven't seen any stinkin' badges. You do need badges, right?" I mocked and heard Richard moan behind me.

"I am Agent Smith and this is Agent Jones," the Latino smiled.

I wasn't sure if they understood my rudeness, or were just ignoring it. Maybe neither of them had ever seen *The Treasure of Sierra Madre*.

"Yeah, I saw the old TV show growing up, *Alias Smith and Jones*. About two cowboy outlaws trying to go straight. Is that what you two are?"

"We didn't come here for a confrontation," Smith said.

"Richard stays?"

"If you want."

I sat down at one of the Nautilus machines. When I turned to Richard he was shaking his head and trying to hide a thin smile. I learned a long time ago that any government agent—ours or theirs—would treat you as inferior and with contempt if you let them. If you didn't let them, they would work slowly upward toward respect when they dealt with you. As long as their guns were holstered, I wasn't going to make it easy for them.

"So, we're not going to have a confrontation. What did you come for?" The idea of seeing a badge forgotten.

"For some reason," Smith finally began, "you have expressed a concern that three of our operatives are involved in a murder."

"This is strictly off the record," Jones yelled. "Right?"

"Right," I said.

"When we received the inquiry on them, we were very concerned." Smith stroked his goatee. "We contacted Chief Dowley immediately and he explained the situation. We looked into it right away."

"Are we talking about Lopez, Gonzales and Fernandez?" I looked toward a mirror image of Smith.

"So you found out Pepe's name," Smith said. "You are resourceful, but I've been told you were."

"We took the accusations seriously." Jones touched his glasses, making sure they were snug on his large nose. "These men are important, and we can't have them doing something outside the law."

"Like murder?" I said.

"Definitely not murder," Smith nodded.

"We're sorry about your friend." Jones had a blank expression as he spoke.

"We got the dates and pertinent information from the Chief and looked into it." Smith nodded some more, and took out a small notebook. "Your friend was attacked on Saturday morning, January 15, probably around sunrise. All three of our agents were in Miami from Friday, the 14th to Sunday the 16th. There was a bachelor party they attended Thursday night and a wedding Saturday afternoon. Half the Miami Cuban population was at the wedding and corroborated their presence."

He scanned some pages and then put the booklet away.

"How come they were drinking in a Key West bar before midnight Saturday night?"

"They weren't," Jones said. "We talked to witnesses in Miami who had breakfast with them Sunday morning."

"So, maybe there are three other Cubans in town with the same names and look just like your agents," I mocked. "Or maybe, a bunch of Miami Cubans are lying for a comrade."

"No," Smith replied calmly. "We're saying your sources are wrong."

I didn't reply. I looked from one man to the other and turned to see Richard still standing behind me.

"Do you know who the men you're accusing are?" asked Jones, as he leaned against a weight machine.

"No." I scanned the mirror images of us.

"Jones!" Smith called his name firmly.

"Is this where you become the good agent and Smith the bad?" I asked. "What agency are you with? CIA? FBI? Or is it something new from Homeland Security?"

"Mick," Richard called my name.

"Richard," I turned to him, "these clowns are telling me nothing and they know it! Tom is dead and the guys who did it work for them. They'd protect them no matter what."

"We would not protect murderers," Jones yelled across the gym.

"Bullshit," I yelled back. "What about Whitey Bulger? Didn't the Boston FBI protect him and his gang while they murdered and ran drugs?"

"That was twenty years ago," Smith said, "and some rogue FBI agents."

"Maybe it was the tip of the iceberg." I was getting nervous with their attitude. "That's what I think."

The room went quiet. I heard Richard move behind me. Smith and Jones stared at each other, but said nothing.

"I need to use the john." I stood. "If you have something to say, tell me when I get back, or I am out of here."

I walked out of the gym, smiled at Richard, and went to the men's room. When I walked back in Richard was sitting on a weight bench and the two feds were still standing.

"May I leave?" I directed my question to Richard.

"What if we can offer you a major exclusive," Smith grinned. "Would that interest you?"

"Almost as much as putting away Tom's murderers." I had no idea what they were talking about.

"Okay," Smith scowled. "You help us and we'll use everything available to us to find out who killed your friend."

"And if it turns out to be the Cubans?"

"Whoever it is, we turn them over to Chief Dowley," Smith

59

said. "But we need your cooperation."

"Ah, the catch." I sat down across from Richard. "What cooperation?"

I didn't know if it was an act or not, but the tension seemed to be building between the two men. Was it the good-cop, bad-cop ploy, or were they undecided on how much and what to tell me? I had no doubt they would play me, if they thought they could. I waited.

"How do we know if we tell you what's going on you won't run with it to CNN or some other media?" Jones asked.

"You don't," I answered honestly. "But, if it's an operation you are controlling and I can't corroborate the facts, no one will use it."

"Afterward, if you cooperate, we'll get you all the corroboration you need," Jones said.

"You think we can do that?" Smith continued to stroke his goatee.

"We need these three guys to get the operation done." Jones cleaned his glasses. "If he continues chasing after them, innocent or not, he can get press, and we're done."

"What do you recommend, Chief? Will he keep his word?" Smith asked Richard.

"Yeah," Richard said without hesitating. "If he gives you his word, he'll keep it. However, he'll expect you to keep yours, too. If not . . . well, he can be like a pit bull."

"Understood." Jones walked to Smith and whispered something to him.

ELEVEN

Smith sat down across from me and scratched his goatee, while Jones stood leaning against a weight machine and fondled his glasses. The silence grew. Smith cleared his throat. Their expressions told me nothing; they were playing me, hoping to keep me away from their agents.

"I'm going out on a limb here," Smith said.

"Not yet, you aren't." I forced a smile.

He carried himself more like the military men I've known than a federal agent. He hadn't wanted to look like the man in charge, but it appeared he was.

"We are hesitant to discuss this with a fellow traveler."

"I didn't know Joe McCarthy had an illegitimate son," I said.

Smith stared angrily at me and then turned to Richard. "You ever read any of his crap?"

"Things he's written since moving here," Richard said.

"If he isn't a communist, he's a socialist." Smith continued to stroke his goatee. "Big supporter of the rebels in El Salvador, the Sandanistas in Nicaragua. Go on the Internet, look for yourself. It's all left-wing shit."

"I didn't support the Contras and they were rebels. What's the point of this? Do we have a deal or not? If we're done I'm leaving." I gave Richard a quick glance, but he was noncommittal.

"Yeah, we've got a deal, I just wanted you to know that we know all about you." Smith stood, moved around the gym, but kept his stare on me. "The men you've accused of murder were military officers in the Cuban army. They defected a year ago, after Castro dropped out of the picture, and the Cuban government doesn't know where they are."

He talked without facial expression, not a smile or frown, or twitch. I don't think his yellow-gray eyes blinked or showed emotion; they looked at me without seeing. But his voice was beginning to hint of excitement.

"They go back to Cuba by boat whenever they want," I said. "Three high-ranking defectors and the Cuban government doesn't know where they are?"

"They don't go back when they want, they go back when we tell them to." Smith stopped pacing for a moment. "There's been plastic surgery, a loss of weight, they look younger and have new identities."

"There's been no press on their defection." Jones sneaked glimpses at the mirrors.

"I am sure the Cubans think we have them, but they don't know, and they must be going crazy wondering why we don't exploit the defection."

"Okay," I said, to stay in the game. "Highly unlikely, but possible."

"When they were picked up by the Coast Guard they were going to be repatriated, but their story was intriguing." Smith paced again. "We were sent to investigate and they told us they were ordered to defect by a popular general and Communist Party official who want to defect, too. We had questions and they had the right answers. We know they were military officers."

Smith waited for a response. I didn't give him one. He might as well have added that he was from military intelligence.

"You following this?" Jones put his glasses back on.

"Yeah. What's in it for them?"

"The general and party official think that now with Castro out of the picture, they can cause enough unrest upon defecting to topple the communist government. There's discontent in the military and party, but anyone that tried anything from within would be shot. They get here, declare their support for a non-Communist Cuba." Smith's tone couldn't hide his excitement.

His pleasure in a subject that could bring the Miami Cuban population from its deathbed to celebrate sounded real.

"They go back after the change, and what?"

"They have enough supporters to take over the government and bring change." Jones pushed his glasses back in place.

"And they will be more favorable to the United States." Smith cracked his knuckles. "They will bring change, democracy and end the bankruptcy Castro brought to the island. And they will have the support of our government."

"And you believe these guys?" I wanted to know what democracy meant to the defectors and their leaders in Havana, but kept my mouth shut. Most Miami exile extremists' idea of democracy was allowing everyone the freedom to agree with them. I was even curious as to what democracy meant to Smith and Jones.

"Yes," Smith said, "they've gone back and brought us proof . . . and don't ask what it is. But when it's over, you'll get to see it first."

"I get to meet the general and party official?" I did not expect an honest reply.

"Whatever it takes to get your cooperation."

"There's something missing, they're smuggling Cubans into the States, they killed Tom, but for what?'

"Exactly what we've been trying to tell you," Smith said. "It doesn't make sense for them to be involved in your friend's murder."

"They expect to be heroes in Cuba by this time next year."

Jones glanced at our mirror images and fixed his glasses. "What do they care about your sailboat race?"

"As far as the smuggling goes, it's their cover in Miami." Smith walked around the gym equipment. "When the Coast Guard picks up rafters we think might be in danger if they're returned, these guys bring them in like smugglers would, and they are heroes in Miami. They aren't getting away with anything."

I couldn't swallow that part, their caring about the safety of Cuban rafters. They probably chose rafters like the slaughterhouse chose cows, without caring one way or another.

"For argument sake, let's say I believe you," I said. "Whenever I work on an article, when I get to a certain point that I have to make a decision on the direction of the story, I ask myself one big question."

I stood up and pulled a handle from one of the weight machines and it caused the weights to rise, and broke the sterile silence of the room. When I let go of the handle, the weights fell loudly. Then the room went silent again.

"What question?" Jones stared at me.

Smith sighed and gave Jones a nasty smirk. He sat across from Richard.

"He always this big a pain in the ass?" Smith asked Richard.

"Usually," Richard glanced at me. "Years ago he would've been a candidate for a rubber hose."

"Some places he'd still be a candidate."

Richard agreed.

"Are you going to keep us here all night or are you going to tell us what this big question is?" Smith stood up.

"What if?" Habit forced me to reach in my pocket for a nonexisting cigar. "What if I am looking at the situation from the wrong direction? What if I am being lied to? What if, I ask myself about all the information I've put together. And most times I find something hiding, something I've overlooked."

"Have you asked yourself 'what if' your sources are lying?"

"Yeah, and I don't think they are. I trust them."

"What if we are going to topple the Cuban regime?" Smith's voice no longer tried to hide his enthusiasm. "Have you asked yourself that? And you'll be the first journalist to break the story . . ."

"The first journalist to interview the defectors?"

"Yes."

"Before the government falls? Let me tell their story, their hopes?"

"If I have that authority," Smith said.

"What authority do you have? Is all this bullshit and a waste of my time? I thought this was your operation."

"What if they don't want to talk to you?"

"They're in your charge," I said. "Don't give 'em a choice."

"Anything else?" Smith sat across from me.

"Yeah, you still have to use your resources to look into Tom's murder, and if your agents did it, they aren't allowed to flee to Cuba."

I didn't believe anything they said, but I had to make myself seem to, so they wouldn't catch my suspicion. If the story had been true, I'd dance naked down Duval Street at noon for the exclusive, and I needed to show that enthusiasm. But, I wouldn't have let Tom's murderers go for the exclusive, and I figured they knew that.

"You have my word on it." Smith forced a smile. "We'll investigate and if they, one or all or any of them, are guilty, Chief Dowley gets them." He turned to Jones.

"You have my word on it, too," Jones lied, and then smiled for the first time. "Have you considered what if this is not about the sailboat race, but is payback for something you did in the past?"

I wondered what they knew of my past, but they probably knew more than I remembered.

"Or, what if it is a group of Miami Cubans? Some of the old guard, for their own reasons, would think arranging the race to Marina Hemingway is treason, and killing you, or anyone involved, was justifiable. It might be very dangerous being you right now." Smith stopped in front of me.

"It seems you've narrowed the killers down to the first Cubans you found," Jones said. "Smith is right, it could be very dangerous for you, especially if it is Miami Cubans. I would be real careful."

I had no doubt Smith and Jones would squash me like a palmetto bug if they thought it would solve their problem and they could get away with it. People like them are the types who keep dictators in power. Human life is expendable, if it will help achieve their goal and keep the status quo. Under other circumstances, they could be happily employed in Cuba.

"How do I monitor your operation? I'd hate to get out of the loop."

"I can't say much, but I can tell you when they arrive it will be in Key West," Smith said. "Chief Dowley will be aware and, I assume, he will keep you informed. The Chief will be the middleman, so we won't have to meet again."

"I trust Richard, if it's okay with him, I agree." I turned and Richard was nodding.

I had lied and been lied to, and as I looked at Richard, I realized I had done it somewhat out of fear, and that bothered me. It wasn't a game to these men, but my whole life had been a game of one kind or another, since my college days; a game that came to its drastic conclusion on a Tijuana street. Or, so I had thought.

"Excuse me, I need to use the john again." I walked out of the gym and wanted to throw up.

I tossed cold water on my face and rubbed my eyes. For the first time I saw flecks of gray in my red hair. I splashed more water on my face and when I stared into the mirror, my green eyes looked dull.

As I walked along the hallway, I passed the dark gym and saw my reflection in the window and it seemed as if I had never been inside the empty room. What had just happened? I wondered as I pushed the door open and walked outside.

TWELVE

A cool, damp breeze swept across the boulevard from Garrison Bight and the tropical tastes and scents of Key West drifted about as I left the police station. The full moon shone in the heavens, crowned by stars, as I turned toward Duval Street. The black water of the bight mirrored the sky. The winter temperature was in the mid-seventies and my old Jeep was the perfect Key West vehicle; with the side and back widows off, the bikini top was enough to keep the two front seats safe from the winter sun and rain.

A secret I don't share often is that after ten at night you can find plenty of free parking at city hall on Angela Street. It's about a half block off the center of Duval Street, so it is always walking distance to most of the bars and restaurants in Old Town.

Routine drove me there, because parking was the last thing on my mind. The evening had begun with the cleaning of my Glock—a reminder of past horrors—and then there had been the Cuban waiting at the marina when I left. He caused me concern I was unable to laugh off. Add Bob and Burt being all gung-ho about tracking down the Cubans and that frightened me, too. Then the call from Richard and my trip to meet two federal agents, who were not what they claimed to be.

I put a Cuban cigar in my pocket, checked to make sure my lighter worked, and walked toward Virgilio's, where I hoped to find some semblance of sanity at midnight, so I could sort through the evening's events.

When I walked in off Applerouth Lane, any narrower and it would be an alley, the Larry Baeder Band was playing Blues at the small inside bar. A doublewide doorway and a large open window allowed the music to fill the patio that was half-packed with people. I found a small table for two near the back wall under a tree, and sat down and lit up the cigar. Virgilio's is a local hangout, but its drink prices keep many of my friends from stopping there. It is hard for anyone living in Key West to go anywhere social and not run into someone they know.

I ordered a Jameson on the rocks and took a long swallow. I stared at the wall next to the brightly lit outdoor bar, sipped the remainder of my drink, and smoked the cigar, as I tried to make some sense out of what had happened.

Even though I didn't like it, I accepted that Richard had led me into the lion's den, like a Christian in old Rome, when he called me to the police station. He could have warned me on what to expect, he could have been more vocal in my support, but instead, he sat close by and remained silent. And, he called me there when the station was all but empty. What did that tell me? I had no viable witness to the meeting. Why? How sure was I that the two men were federal agents? If I doubted Richard's loyalty, I had to doubt their identity.

I didn't believe Smith or Jones. How can you believe two guys who took their pseudonyms from an old TV Western? Would Paladin be the next agent I met? It didn't feel right to me, and I had benefited in the past by listening to my feelings. They were obviously trying to protect the *gusanos*. But why?

Could Tom have known them from his trips to Cuba? That thought made me sit up. The *gusanos* had been here for about a year, Smith and Jones said. Tom had been sailing to Cuba for more than twenty years and seemed to know everyone at the marina and the surrounding neighborhoods. I first met Tom when Bob introduced me to him at Marina Hemingway, seven years ago. I had to sail the ninety miles to Cuba to meet someone from Key West. Could Tom have recognized them, even with plastic surgery? For that matter, had there been plastic surgery? What were they protecting that was worth killing for? Could it really involve the overthrow of the Cuban government?

I ordered another drink while I listened to the music and the excited late-night chatter between couples, and smiled at a few people I recognized.

Cuban cigars, some people tout, are no longer the best cigars in the world, but I think the Cuban "Romeo and Julieta Churchill" is the best, and I was smoking one. It burnt slow and the ash held, and there was good Blues music soothing the patio customers.

No matter how hard I tried, it was difficult for me to remember Tom, as I'd known him all these years. Instead, I saw the horribly disfigured man at the sail club, who died this morning.

"Are you waiting for someone?" Padre Thomas stood next to my table.

I looked up from my reverie and he was there in his old shirt, faded shorts, and quietly waited for me to offer him a seat. He looked cold. I pushed the empty chair away from the table for him.

"Do you want a beer, Padre?"

"Please."

I ordered him a Bud and a fresh drink for myself.

"What brings you to Virgilio's?"

"You," he said as our drinks arrived.

I looked at my watch and it was almost one.

"Me?"

"Yeah, I was worried about you. I waited at the marina and someone told me they thought they saw you coming in here."

"Why would you worry about me?"

He lit a Camel. "I think your life is in danger."

He said it flatly, without emotion, but gave me a concerned look.

I stared at him and smiled. "You could be right, Padre. Two guys who said they were federales thought I was in danger, too." I stuck the cigar in my mouth. "I think it was meant as a threat."

"And?" There was still concern in his voice.

"And that's what I am sitting here thinking about."

"You don't look worried."

"I'm confused, Padre, I'm scared, I don't have time to worry, not yet, anyway."

"Can I help?"

"What do the angels say?" I took the cigar out of my mouth. "Can't they protect me?"

"You should be careful, Mick." He lit another cigarette.

The band stopped playing and some of the couples from the bar and patio began to leave. It was getting close to closing time.

"I plan on being very careful, Padre. And you can tell the angels I am working on justice for the three Cubans." I sipped my drink.

"If there is anything I can do . . ." he left the sentence unfinished.

"Have you ever killed anyone, Thomas?" I sat up straight waiting for his answer.

"Why would you ask me that?" His expression remained unchanged, but his searching eyes were intense. "What would make you think I'd ever killed anyone?"

"You could have been in Vietnam."

"Oh, I hadn't thought of that. I was in the seminary during that war."

"Lucky you."

"But you've killed."

"Yes. I've killed one too many people, Padre, and I thought it was over," I confessed. "Now I am not so sure."

"There's a difference between killing and murder. I don't think you are capable of murder."

"It's a thin line that's easy to cross." I took a long swallow of my Jameson and puffed on what remained of my cigar. I thought of the times in California when my rage drove me to the edge and murder was possible.

Thomas drank his beer, smoked his cigarette. "Are you going back to the marina now?"

"No." I smiled. I didn't want him hanging around, I had things to work out. "I'm gonna walk up Duval."

"You shouldn't be alone." He crushed out the stub of his cigarette.

"I won't be, Padre," I lied, "I'm waiting on a young lady."

He looked around and then finished his beer. "Be careful, Mick, and thank you for the beer," and he walked away.

As I paid my tab, I wondered if he'd wait outside and follow me on his bike.

"Where you off to, Mick?" Larry Baeder said as I passed by the indoor bar.

"The Tree Bar. I'm meeting a girl."

Nice thing about telling a guy that line is he won't want to tag along, usually. Larry is married and he may enjoy a drink or two after a gig, but he always wants to get home.

"We're playing the Hog end of next week. See you there?"

"You know it. Opening Thursday or Friday?"

"Thursday."

"See you Thursday night," and I walked out onto Applerouth Lane.

A much younger crowd hung around outside the bar across the lane in small groups. Loud, recorded music from the bar violated the night. I thought how I'd lied more in the last few hours than I had in months. Lied to friends like Thomas and Larry, and it came as second nature. Lied and was lied to, I thought as I wandered along Duval, mixed in with the dirty-and-smelly Rainbow Children carrying worn backpacks and blankets and their dogs, and tourists who had had too much to drink, but the bars were still open, so they had room for a few more beers. Cars leisurely worked their way on Duval as frantic scooter riders dashed along the busy street; revelers jaywalked and horns blared. Rap music bounced out of open car windows and Spanish love songs competed for attention from other cars.

The air was cool and millions of stars were still blinking around the moon. In Boston, it was snowing and in Los Angeles, it was smoggy and the streets weren't safe at closing time. Crime in Key West only became crime after a person lived here a few years; before that, it was mostly laughable. There are no gang-related, drive-by shootings, and the cops know most of the small-time drug dealers. What would pass as pranks in Boston and LA made the local crime report in Key West. Then, of course, some animal would find his or her way to Key West and kill for no logical reason, and someone good like Tom would die. Most were caught and sent to prison, because the city cops and county sheriffs were professionals, and murder wasn't good for tourism.

Yuppies and wannabe reggae kings and queens spilled out of Jimmy Buffett's Margaritaville club. They were trying to exist in the nirvana that Buffett had created in his music, refusing to believe it was a fantasy world that eluded all, including Jimmy. Boisterous laughter wafted from the ground floor of the Bull, a bar with large, gaping windows that opened toward Duval; the second-floor porch of the Whistle Bar, upstairs from the Bull, was full of partyers yelling and whistling at the small packs of young girls walking by. A light dusting of sweet marijuana smoke skipped by on the breeze, as I made my way along the busy street.

Loud alternative rock from Durty Harry's forced its way up the brick-lined alley to the rustic Tree Bar. Rick, the ex–New York cop turned bartender, raised a bottle of Jameson as I looked at the bar, and I nodded. He placed my glass by Tita Toledo and I used it as an excuse to sit next to her.

Tita and I had dated recently. She's thirty, with bronze skin and bright green eyes, unusual for a Puerto Rican, and a face that reminded me of a young Sophia Loren. Her hair is long and blacker than midnight. I knew her brother Paco when I was at Harvard, and met her when she was much too young for me to even think about. She didn't look anything like her brother, but she was still his kid sister.

"How come you are not with *los locos?*" she smiled.

"I left them here a few hours ago." I sipped my Jameson's.

"They are at Schooner and acting stranger than normal." She drank her vodka tonic. "They get stranger every time I see them. I thought you would be at the captain's meeting."

I'd forgotten the evening's captain's meeting to arrange the taking of Tom's ashes to the Gulf.

"What were Bob and Burt doing?"

"First they argued against taking Tom's ashes out in speedboats," she laughed. "They said he was a sailor."

"And?"

"They were overruled. There are about twenty-five captains going, so the sailors were invited to go in the speedboats."

"What's strange about that?"

"They were just louder than usual and smoking cigars and putting the ashes in plastic cups." She took another sip of her drink. "They are up to no good. And they were drinking tequila shots."

"Ouch! They are not tequila drinkers."

We sat quietly, nursed our drinks, and turned our backs to the bar to watch the circus parade on the street. Cars and scooters fought for space as the corner light by Sloppy Joe's turned from green to red.

"Where were you?"

"I was with Richard at the police station."

"Everything okay?"

"I think so," I lied, again. "What are you doing?"

"Looking for you," she smiled. "I've missed you."

"I'm honored."

"No, you're drunk and you shouldn't be driving."

"I'm walking halfway."

"I can take you home on my scooter." She turned to look at me. "This is only my second drink."

"I need to be on the boat tonight, why don't you come there?"

"I'm working tomorrow."

"Bring a change of clothes."

"Why can't you ever stay with me? You afraid of sleeping on dry land?" She turned away. "Or are you still afraid of Paco?"

"Paco," I laughed. "Bring a change of clothes and I'll meet you at my boat."

"I'll see how I feel when I get home." She finished her drink.

Her scooter was in the taxi zone. She smiled, but moved before I could lean in and kiss her, and drove off.

"I guess Tita's on your tab," Rick said as he went to refill my glass.

"No more," I stopped him from pouring a new drink. "What did she have?"

"Four drinks, she'd been waiting here for two hours."

I paid for our drinks and laughed at the lie she told about how many drinks she had. The night had been one long lie. I crossed the street and walked slowly back to the Jeep.

It always amazed and frightened me how busy Key West

streets are at two in the morning. Scooters and bicycles are the most dangerous at that hour. Bikes without lights and scooters that refuse to obey traffic laws any time of day or night, zip between cars without regard for safety or sanity. It is a tribute to Key West drivers that someone on a bike or scooter wasn't killed hourly.

The marina was dark and quiet. I got out of the Jeep, leaned against the rail, and looked out toward the houseboats, floating homes and sailboats as they bobbed in the black water. The winter breeze still whistled through the masts and the moon had moved west and would be gone soon. It seemed to be a peaceful end to a chaotic evening. I thought of Tita and realized I really wanted her to come to the boat. I hurried toward my dock because I didn't want her to see the Glock on the chart table.

I noticed the light at the dock's entrance had burned out again and thought nothing of it as I headed down the ramp, until a bright silent flash blinded me and forced me to reach toward an ache in my head. Then the light faded and it went dark, like in a dream, and I was falling in slow motion through the blackness; suddenly I was wet, but I continued to fall, and then the darkness became absolute.

THIRTEEN

I became aware of the horizon as a soft light exposed it from the darkness. I was no longer falling. I was motionless. The horizon began to fade as the light brightened. A soft humming echoed from the light. I thought about the stories people told after being revived from death, about how God appeared as a bright, comforting light and they were drawn to it; they wanted to go to the light, they often said, and were disappointed when they were told to return to their body.

The light wasn't warm or comforting and I didn't hear God, only a humming, and it didn't feel like my soul had left my body. Did God hum?

There was nothing but the light and the humming, and the annoying humming was getting louder as the light continued to get brighter. Dull gray images began passing through the light and my breathing became difficult. The darker the images became the harder it was for me to breathe.

For the first time I felt panic. The light blinded me and I tried to push myself up so I could breathe. I couldn't move. The images became larger and darker, and I feared the obscurity they threatened. I felt myself trying to suck air into my burning lungs as the light began to fade and the images became larger.

"God!" I screamed, thinking He was leaving as the light faded and the darkness grew.

My eyes opened and I was startled to see Norm Burke, my friend from Los Angeles, leaning over me, and Doctor Gayle

Mellow standing next to him. We called her Dr. G. I'd spent enough time in emergency rooms to know where I was, but Norm couldn't be there. What was he doing there? What was I doing there?

Dr. G said something to Norm and he pushed the white curtain aside and walked away.

"Mick," Dr. G said, "can you hear me?"

I nodded as I watched Norm leave.

"Say something."

"Who . . . why am I here?" The words fumbled from my mouth.

I looked around the hygienic room, waiting for her reply.

"The paramedics brought you in from the marina." She lifted my hand and took my pulse. "Your friends called them."

"Did I have a heart attack?" It was all I could think of.

"You'd need a heart first," Norm laughed as he pushed the white curtain aside and walked in, followed by another man. I hadn't heard the crusty laugh in years and it helped ease my panic.

"This is Dr. Latour, Mick," Dr. G said.

He was young, with light brown hair, a pale complexion, and tired brown eyes. He held a clipboard and looked down at it.

"Head hurt?" he asked.

"Yeah." I realized how badly it hurt. "Norm?"

"I liked it better when you called me God. You're gonna be okay."

"Thank you," Dr. Latour snapped. "I'll give a second opinion, if you'll both wait outside."

After Dr. G and Norm left, the young doctor poked and prodded and I think I passed everything accept when he asked me what day it was.

"Wednesday."

"Early Thursday morning, very early," he said in a sour voice.

"You should stay in the hospital until tomorrow, so we can watch you. You have a concussion, but seem to be all right otherwise. A concussion can be . . ."

"I have my nurse here," I said, accepting Norm was there, and watched the doctor's face twitch.

"Dr. Mellow said you wouldn't stay. I am recommending you stay, but do what you want. I have other patients that need and want my attention." He scribbled something on the papers on the clipboard and began to walk out.

"Why is it you always piss off doctors?" Norm held the curtain open for the doctor to leave.

"What are you doing here?" I forced my legs over the side of the bed.

I realized I was wearing a backless hospital gown. I tried to hide the dizziness I felt as I sat up.

"What I am doing here is bringing you some clothes." He pulled a small bag from a chair.

I still didn't know what had happened, but felt too dizzy to make sense out of anything. I stood up slowly and dressed, as Norm handed me my clothes.

"These are mine." I slipped into a pair of old frayed shorts.

"You certainly wouldn't fit into my shorts, hoss," Norm drawled. "I'm staying on the boat. I guess we're roommates again."

"What's going on, Norm?" I sat in the chair to slip on my flip-flops. "Why are you here?"

"When we get outside," he said as Dr. G walked in.

"He goes with you, Norm," Dr. G said, as if they were old friends and I wasn't there. "I hold you responsible for him."

"I've been babysitting this bum for almost twenty years, Doctor. I will make him behave and bring him to your office Monday morning."

"You call my cell if anything seems strange. And be in my office at eight sharp, no later."

"You're the doctor," he saluted.

"I'm glad one of you realizes it." She turned to me. "Is he as good as he says?"

"He's pulled me through worse than this." I wondered when she had given Norm her cell number. "I trust him."

"You are trusting him with your life." She gave me a puzzled look.

And, I thought to myself, it wasn't the first time, but I had hoped after the last time that it would never happen again.

"I think you should stay," she said.

I shook my head and it hurt, so I stopped. "Norm's a good nurse."

"Okay," Dr. G sighed. "I've signed you out, but you need to wait for the orderly to wheel you to the parking lot. It is the hospital's policy."

"And a necessary one," Norm said. "We'll wait."

Dr. G smiled her best bedside smile at Norm. She's a big woman with a tender touch, warm hands and a clear, teenager's complexion; her blue eyes twinkle and she is quick to laugh, but in those few moments when she is stern, you listen and believe her.

"I suppose you are responsible for a few of those scars on Mick's body," she said in her stern mode.

"He earned them on his own, Dr. G, but I am responsible for patching up a few of the holes."

"He's responsible," I moaned.

She shook her head and tried to hide a smile as she turned to walk out. "Two guys still trying to be Peter Pan," she said loud enough for us to hear.

"She's a good person, and she likes you."

"What's not to like?" I stood slowly. "Are we going?"

Norm stuck his head out the curtain and waved me forward.

"Screw the rules." He walked away.

The emergency room was busy with nurses at stations writing or reading forms and the brightness reminded me of my dream, or whatever it was. Patients sobbed and cried out from behind closed curtains. Norm slowed his walk to accommodate me. We moved unnoticed, and wandered through the large double doors to the lifeless waiting room that reminded me of childhood images of purgatory. As normal, the room was full of grim-looking people and kids waiting endlessly for help. Someone I took to be one of the city's many homeless men sat at the intake window and his dirty, bearded chin kept falling to his chest as the nurse tried to get information from him. The other intake window was empty.

"That's a depressing place." Norm held the exit door open for me.

"Have you ever seen an emergency room that wasn't? Makes me think of purgatory."

"I wouldn't know about that," he lied.

The sun hadn't risen yet and the gray pre-dawn was cool. The parking lot was almost empty and it made me wonder how everyone had gotten there. I saw my Jeep and followed Norm to it. He held the door for me and I painfully lifted myself into the passenger seat.

"Are you hungry?"

"No." My voice was a whisper. My head hurt and I was dizzy.

Norm slid into the driver's seat and shook the small bag that had held my clothes.

"Medication." We drove out of the parking lot. "But you need to eat first."

"I have cottage cheese on the boat."

"Coffee, too?"

"Yeah, Cuban coffee."

I must have fallen asleep because Norm shook me when we

were at the marina.

"Sleeping ain't a good idea right now, Mick, let's get that coffee."

I took my time getting out of the Jeep. The light above the dock ramp was still out and I walked slowly to the railing. I held on to it and looked down at the black water and it sent chills up my spine.

"What happened, Norm?"

"You have no idea." He stood next to me.

"Not if it wasn't a heart attack." My head hurt too bad to think.

"Someone tried to kill you."

I turned and leaned against the railing, but couldn't relate to his comment.

"How do you know that?"

"Let's get that coffee." He held my shoulder and moved me toward the ramp to the dock. "I'll tell you all about it. It's been a long and strange night, hoss."

Fourteen

It took a long, silent walk down the floating docks to reach the *Fenian Bastard*. My boat has a solid safety rail around it, and as I looked at her, I knew it was going to hurt to climb aboard. Norm went first and, as I climbed the three steps to the boat, he held his hand out to steady me as I went over the rail.

Padre Thomas was asleep in the cockpit. He wore one of my T-shirts and a pair of my faded jeans. His presence startled me as I stepped onto the deck. Norm shook him awake.

"Mick," Thomas said, rubbing his eyes, "are you okay?"

"Thomas? What are you doing here?"

Aromas of coffee came from the main hatch. I sat down as Norm went below.

"He pulled your sorry ass out of the water, and made coffee, too," Norm yelled from below. "Still take it black with two sugars?"

"Yeah," I said. "Thomas, what happened?"

Norm carried up three cups of coffee and sat down.

"Tell him." He handed us the coffee.

"I warned you," Thomas reminded me, as he sipped the coffee. "I warned him earlier," he said to Norm

"I know, but what happened?" The coffee smelled good.

"A guy came out of the mangroves as you walked down the ramp, and whacked you with a two-by-four," Thomas whispered, excitedly. "He swung it like a baseball bat and you went over the railing into the water."

I looked at Norm, who was trying to hide a smirk.

"How do you know?" I sipped my coffee.

"I was over at the seawall on Roosevelt, waiting for you. I yelled, but you mustn't have heard me."

"Who was it?"

"I don't know," he frowned. "The guy looked down at you and walked away. I jumped in and swam to you. I tried to get you out, but the water's too deep, so I yelled for help, and Norm came."

I looked at Norm, again.

"I didn't see a thing." He raised his arm in surrender. "I heard the yelling and came out to see what was going on and when I didn't see anyone . . ."

"I kept yelling," Thomas said.

"Yeah, he did. I walked toward the yelling and there you two were. If he hadn't gotten to you when he did, you would've drowned."

We drank coffee in silence. I couldn't remember falling into the water, but I did remember the sudden flash of pain in my head.

"Thank you," I said to Thomas between sips. "I don't remember any of it, especially being in the water."

"By the time I helped pull you out, some of your neighbors had called 911. The EMTs arrived and off you went to the hospital."

"I went with Norm to the hospital and I brought back your wet clothes. I took a taxi here and changed into some of your dry clothes. I hope you don't mind."

I looked at Thomas. His eyes were red, and he looked tired.

"I don't mind, keep the clothes."

Norm carried our empty cups below.

"Padre Thomas, go home and get some sleep, Norm is here, and I am all right. Thank you, again, Padre, but please keep this between us and don't tell anyone."

I needed to talk to Norm, and I knew he wouldn't open up in front of Thomas; it was going to be hard enough to get him to tell me the truth.

"I warned you, Mick. You should have believed me."

"I believed you, Padre, I just wasn't ready."

"If you need anything call me, and I won't tell anyone. Let me help, if I can." He stood up to go and hesitated.

"Mick, it's not over," he whispered. "Your friend, Norm, has an evil side to him, but . . . you're his good side, so let him help . . . but be careful."

I turned slowly and watched him climb down to the dock.

"How do you know about Norm?"

"The angels know," and he walked away.

I watched as he moved slowly along the dock toward the parking lot and wondered if luck had anything to do with Thomas being at the seawall.

"Hey," Norm called to get my attention. He handed me another cup of coffee. "That guy is your guardian angel."

I burst out laughing and couldn't control myself for at least a minute. It hurt my head, I laughed so hard.

"I'm glad you can laugh." He sat down.

"You don't know how funny that is," I stopped laughing. "But you may be right."

I would wait for the right opportunity to tell Norm the story about Padre Thomas and the angels.

The sun began to rise and the sky turned shades of purple and pink above the homes in New Town. We sat and watched the stars fade as the sky turned to reds and yellows and daylight pushed the darkness away. Pelicans and seagulls sailed through the sky and squawked their greetings. Traffic began to build on North Roosevelt Boulevard as the island stretched to meet the new day.

"What are you doing here?"

"I have two fighters on a card at the Indian casino near Miami . . ." He stopped and looked at my pinched up frown. "Oh, you mean the truth?"

"For a change."

"I do have two fighters on the weekend card at the casino. Actually, since you've been gone from LA, I've pretty much retired from the adventurous life and been a real trainer and boxing promoter."

"Good for you." I did not believe him. Norm is a career government-agency man, but I have never been able to figure out what agency, and he usually denies it. "Now the truth."

"So, what was it, two weeks ago?" he stopped and pretended to think. "About that. I get a call: 'Your friend Murphy has surfaced again and he's gonna fuck up a mission.' Well, I am surprised as hell it's taken you this long to stick your nose where it ain't appreciated."

"I surfaced. What have I been, underwater? What are you here to do?"

"Officially, to keep you from screwing up an operation called 'Coconut Telegraph.' "

"It's a Jimmy Buffett song."

"Mick, I never said they were clever, not even when I worked for them. You're apparently screwing with operatives that are important to this agency and they have asked me to intervene."

"They murdered my friend. And, they're not going to get away with it. Intervene all you want." I finished my coffee. "What are you planning to do?"

"I don't know." He went to get more coffee. "Steer you away from them, get you involved in something else, I don't know. I figured I'd get your take on whatever's happening. No more coffee," he handed me the last full cup.

"You know, Norm, in the last twelve hours everyone I've

talked to has lied to me, including someone I thought wouldn't lie to me; and me, I've lied to almost everyone I've met during that time and, like that's not enough to make the day suck, some asshole has tried to kill me."

"Well, it kind of makes you believe things can only improve from here on, don't it?" he smiled. "Now it's your turn. Tell me the truth."

I was no longer tired, but I didn't feel too steady. I went below, mixed some cottage cheese and fruit together, and ate. Norm sat at the hatch as I told him about Tom's murder, the sailboat race, connecting the three Cubans to the murder, and meeting Smith and Jones. Afterward, he handed me two small bottles of pills from the hospital. One was for dizziness and one for pain. I swallowed one of each with a swig of water.

"Other than what the bartender Lu heard, what other evidence do you have?" he said, as I came back up on deck.

It was too early, and I was too dizzy, to tell him about the angels and my deal with Thomas.

"You need to trust me on this one, for a while, but I have something."

I couldn't believe I said it so straightforward. Maybe I was beginning to really believe in the angels.

"I don't think I know Smith or Jones, not from your description. You know that's not their real names, right?"

"No shit! They lied to me?"

"Okay, I may deserve that, but it's been a while since we've done this kind of shit!"

"And I wish we were not doing it now. What is it we're doing?"

"I've got to find a way to do my job and keep you out of trouble at the same time. First, you stay quiet for a day or two, while I find out who Smith and Jones really are and what agency they're working for."

"And then?"

"We take small steps, hoss," he drawled. "If they have the ability to corrupt a local Chief of Police, they could be some real bad hombres, and we don't wanna lock horns with them until we know more."

FIFTEEN

I didn't like the idea of hanging around for a couple of days while Norm searched for the identities of Smith and Jones, but I wasn't sure what I could accomplish feeling the way I did. I had to call Bob and Burt and let them know what had happened and hoped they'd reconsider their idea of helping.

"Where are you going?" I said when Norm joined me on deck.

"I should be able to do everything from Miami in a day or two. Do you need anything before I leave?"

"The Glock. I didn't see it below."

"I put it in our hiding place in the bilge. I was surprised to find it on the chart table."

Years ago, Norm had built a watertight box for me that fit firmly into a narrow space between the cabin deck and the small bilge on the *Fenian Bastard*. He sized it to hold the Glock, extra clips and a stack of money. On a quick search of the boat, the box would be difficult to find.

"It's been in its hiding place since Panama. I cleaned it last night."

"You did a good job, it's clean." He went to get it.

From where I sat, I could see the floating dock, and as Norm got up, I saw Bob, Burt, and Tita walking toward us.

"Not right now. Company's coming."

Norm turned toward the dock.

"Friends of yours?"

"Bob and Burt."

"And the young lady is?"

"Tita, a friend."

"Your class of friends is improving," he smiled. "She someone special?"

I let the comment go without answering.

Bob and Burt looked like I felt, then I remembered Tita telling me they were doing tequila shots at Schooner last night. Tita carried a plastic Albertson's bag and prodded them along from behind.

"They get seasick easily?"

"They're my sailing buddies."

Norm looked from me to them and then back at me.

"I must be missing something."

"They were doing tequila shots last night at the captain's meeting about Tom's burial at sea. They ain't tequila drinkers."

"Obviously."

"Are you okay?" Tita asked as they climbed aboard.

"Jesus, Mick, we're sorry," Bob and Burt muttered in unison.

They stopped when they saw Norm, then they nodded to him and sat.

"This is my friend Norm from California." Everyone exchanged greetings.

I wondered if they remembered any of my stories about Norm and my misadventures.

"I came by last night and Padre Thomas said you had an accident and were at the hospital," Tita said. "They wouldn't tell me anything at the emergency room, so I finally went home. Are you okay?"

"Yeah. I went off the pier into the water. I thought you worked today."

I wanted to tell Bob and Burt the truth, but not in front of Tita.

"I couldn't go in to work without any sleep." She hesitated and then said, "I told you, you were drunk."

"I should have listened. Where'd you pick these two up at?"

"They were trying to sleep it off at Burt's." She raised the plastic bag in the air. "I told you they were headed toward trouble last night."

"I'm a little slow right now, Tita. What's in the bag?"

"Tom," Bob almost belched.

"Yeah, we took his ashes last night," Burt mumbled.

I looked at Tita for an explanation.

"Your buddies swiped Tom's ashes from the funeral home last night. They found an empty urn and put Tom's ashes in it, and then put their cigar ashes into his urn."

"You what?" It even surprised me.

"Mick, the boaters are gonna take Tom's ashes out in a speedboat this weekend." Bob massaged his forehead.

"We were pissed," Burt said. "We knew you would be, too, if you had been there."

If I thought about it, he was probably right. "Guys, it's not Tom, he's gone, they're only ashes."

"They're Tom's ashes, what's left of our friend, and his last trip on the water should be on a sailboat, not a speedboat." Bob stared at me. "Tell me you don't agree."

"If they were your ashes, Mick, I'd want to take them out on a sailboat," Norm added his two cents, and instantly made friends.

"See," Burt accepted Norm's support. "Getting in the funeral home was easy, the back door was open."

"So it's not like we broke in. We were there to pay our respects and . . . well, one thing led to another . . ." Bob kept rubbing his temples.

"And you don't think anyone is gonna notice?"

"It's windy, Mick. When they turn the urn upside down, the

ashes will blow away. It's not like opening a coffin and seeing the wrong body." Burt stood up and leaned over the railing, as if he was going to be sick.

"He's got a point," Norm said.

"What do you expect to do with the ashes now?" I wanted to know.

"We figure the tide is with us and we'll all go out and spread Tom's ashes in the Gulf Stream. Get it done now, before the weekend." Bob finished rubbing his temples, but still looked in pain.

"Like we'd want you to do for us," Burt said.

"I've got a concussion and you two look like shit. How do you plan to do this? As soon as we pass the reef you'll be chummin' the fish from the rail."

"They've pretty much emptied their stomachs on the way here," Tita frowned.

"Great," I sighed.

"Do you sail, Tita?" Norm asked.

"Yes. Do you?"

"I sailed the *Fenian Bastard* from California to Panama. So, what do you think, could we get these mutineers and thieves to the Gulf Stream and back?"

"Head south from Key West Harbor and you can't miss it. Do you really want to?"

"If we don't get rid of the evidence, your two friends could go to jail and the rest of us are probably guilty of something for not turning them in. Co-conspirators after the fact, at least."

"I like this guy," Bob said.

"Yeah," Burt agreed.

"Me, too," Tita smiled.

Maybe it was the idea of sailing on a beautiful day, but I suddenly felt better as Norm went below and checked the engine fluids, and Tita unhooked the shore power. Bob and Burt sucked down a cold bottle of Coke and two Dramamine tablets, and then, slowly, helped Tita untie the lines. Norm started the engine, checked the gauges, and pointed to the tiller. I shook my head no. I am not often the guest on sails, so I was enjoying myself.

"Here comes Padre Thomas," Tita yelled. "Should we wait for him?"

Thomas was running down the floating dock, waving his hands, still in my T-shirt and jeans.

"No!" Bob said. "No priest, no angels!"

"Yes." I had Norm put the engine in neutral.

"Padre Thomas, I thought you were going home for some rest." I was surprised to see him back at the boat.

"I wanted to go along for the funeral," he winked. "May I?"

"Sure," I said, "jump on, we're pulling out."

Thomas took a seat by Norm.

"How'd you know about this?" Norm had a puzzled look on his face.

"It's hard to keep secrets in Key West," Thomas smiled toward Bob and Burt.

Norm prepared to back the *Fenian Bastard* out, accepting Thomas's answer.

"She still back up like crap?"

"Yeah."

The *Fenian Bastard* is berthed at the third slip from the end of the dock and that allowed her to back out easily into a wide basin. If the tide was going out, the stern was pulled into the basin and the bow headed into the channel; if the tide was coming in, it pushed the stern into the channel, away from the basin, but the bow ended up pointing toward the channel marker, and off she went.

"Tide's going out," I said, as we began moving backward. "She'll back into the basin, just guide her."

"I remember." Norm let her go with the tide.

Most of the channel out of Garrison Bight to Key West Harbor is man-made because of the shallows around the Keys, making it important to sail between the red and green markers. The *Fenian Bastard* draws almost six-feet, so following the marked channel is especially important. We motored through the cut between Hilton Haven on starboard, a residential area, and the military housing on our portside. Norm followed the clear turquoise water of the channel toward Fleming Key, a Spartan military property. A bridge at Fleming Key connects it to the mainland, but it doesn't do a sailboat any good. American Special Forces and Navy SEALs train on Fleming Key and old ammunition bunkers dot its narrow center.

The morning sky was pale blue and cotton-ball clouds danced across it. The salty wind was slow and came from the east, but there was promise it would pick up. The current was strong in the clear, now blue-green water. Tita raised the mainsail as Norm turned the *Fenian Bastard* to follow Fleming Key's coastline. We sailed slowly past the city's mooring field, watching the boats bob in the breeze, and heard the ringing of lines and halyards hitting masts. The bottom was sandy and clear, and according to the depth finder, we were in ten feet of water.

At the end of Fleming Key, the narrow channel cuts between small mangrove islands. Tita took the tiller and made the transition into the harbor, because she was familiar with the channel. Two large cruise ships filled the skyline at Pier B, behind the Westin Hotel. Across from the ships was desolate Christmas Tree Island, with all its invasive pine trees and homeless encampments, surround by anchored boats, and across from it was Sunset Key, where vacant lots cost one million dollars. If Key West is anything, it is a contradiction of lifestyles.

"A walking contradiction, partly truth, partly fiction," a line from an old Kris Kristofferson song went. It applied to everyone in Key West, especially those of us on the *Fenian Bastard*.

Sunset Key was called Tank Island for years and is man made from when the military dredged the Key West channel during World War II so that Navy supply ships could make it into port. Tank Island received its name because it was used as a fuel depot at that time. Today, a section of the island has exclusive Westin guest cottages and the rest are private residences. The new colony also blocks the view of sunset from Mallory Pier.

Bob and Burt were feeling better and as we passed the cruise ships Tita called for the jib to be unfurled. The wind increased to ten knots as we sailed away from Key West, and the *Fenian Bastard*'s sails filled nicely. Tita sailed toward the reef under a port tack, and a school of dolphins played in our wake. The air was cool and refreshing, and Bob brought everyone a cold can of Coke from below. We all needed caffeine. Tita stayed on the tiller, a smile brightening her already excited green eyes.

We passed Sand Key Lighthouse, marking the reef we were heading for, still under a port tack at six knots, while the dolphins crisscrossed before the bow. Padre Thomas sat quietly, staring at the playful school of mammals and the horizon. The dolphins were a good sign and we were all feeling better. Bob and Burt looked more alive than dead, finally. My dizziness had gone and I even took the tiller for the last half hour of the sail.

The shallow, turquoise water around the reef changed to a dark blue the farther we sailed into the Gulf Stream. The boat's depth finder went from readings of ten, to twelve, to twenty feet, to one hundred feet soon after we passed the reef. Finally, the depth finder stopped working, because the water was too deep for a reading.

Tita sat next to me, squeezed my hand, and smiled.

"How did you fall in?"

"It's a long story." I gave a quick glance toward Thomas.

"You've told me some stories about your past with Norm.

The accident had something to do with Tom's death? Is that why Norm is here?"

"Last night, I didn't know Norm was here."

"But you knew he was coming."

"No, I didn't, but now it makes sense. I told you before, I thought this was all behind me."

"I'm glad you're okay." She let go of my hand and checked her watch. "We're in the Gulf Stream."

Tita got the urn and Norm took the tiller, turned the engine on, and pointed the *Fenian Bastard* into the wind. The sails flapped loudly in the background. It was the sound the burial needed. Tom would have understood, it was a proper tune for his funeral dirge. The sun filled the sky and two-foot waves tossed the boat.

The five of us walked to the stern. Bob held the urn and I removed the top and dropped it into the water. We looked at each other as Bob turned the urn over and the ashes and bone chips blew across the waves. When Bob let the urn go, it smacked the water and tossed about in the choppy waves.

"Should we say something?" Bob asked.

"Was he religious?" Burt asked.

"All sailors are," I said.

The urn sank and Tom's ashes were swallowed into the waves.

"I would like to say a few words," Padre Tomas blessed himself. "Lord, please welcome our friend Tom Hunter to your heavenly feast, forgive him his sins on earth because his kindnesses and caring for others benefited so many. Let Tom enjoy the peace of your blessings and receive the rewards of heaven, amen."

"And help us get the bastards who killed him," Burt prayed.

"Amen," Bob said.

"Amen," I said.

"If there is a God," Bob said.

"There has to be, for people like Tom, and because there is a God, there is a hell for the people who killed him." Padre Thomas was no longer praying.

"Let's help 'em get to hell real soon," Burt said.

Tita was silent during the burial and when I walked to her, a tear rolled down her cheek.

"You guys are pathetic." She walked forward to the cockpit.

I didn't think the tear was for Tom.

Sixteen

Norm remained on the tiller as the *Fenian Bastard* swung around to fill the sails, and we headed home. Tita's comments baffled me, but it wasn't the first time I didn't understand her. It was a quiet sail, with the rail hugging the dark-blue water of the Gulf Stream all the way to Sand Key; Tom's death was still on our minds.

"Damn, the bottom is close." Norm looked over the side.

"It's the reef," Tita said, as she let out the mainsail to slow us down.

We were sailing a starboard tack in fifteen feet of clear, emerald-green water. The varying shapes and sizes of the reef, along with the medley of colorful tropical fish caught our attention as we moved over it. No matter how many times I've sailed or snorkeled the reef, it always surprises; sometimes I've seen nurse sharks, once a hammerhead, and always colorful tropical fish. In some locations, the reef is ten feet from the surface, with hidden nooks and crannies that make snorkeling in the shallow water an adventure, even if all you witness are the fish and exotic underwater plants.

Bob brought us beers, and no one seemed to mind that it was only noon.

"Are you staying for a while, Norm?" Tita asked, with a side-glance at me.

"As long as the beer's free. I've got business in Miami, but I hope to come back afterward."

"What business?" Tita held her beer, but didn't drink.

"I've got fighters on the weekend card at the Hard Rock Casino. You should all come, be my guests."

"Could we?" Bob asked.

"Sounds like fun." Burt sipped his beer.

"Mick," Norm turned to me, "you feel up to it?"

"Why not?"

"You, too, Padre." Norm scanned the water ahead as he talked.

"Weekends are very busy for me, but thank you."

I guessed that Padre Thomas didn't approve of the sport. He had seen his fill of bloodletting while a missionary in Central America.

The dolphins had continued on their journey when we stopped for the burial, and the water seemed sadder without them jumping in our wake. We scanned in all directions, but they were gone.

"What class fighters are they?" Bob asked.

"Both are welterweights, South American boys, and tough."

"Championship material?" Burt stood at the rail, enjoying the view and the sunshine.

"Possibly, if they do well this weekend."

The sun helped warm the air and we were in shirtsleeves, trying to soak up as much winter warmth as possible, while it lasted.

"I had a cousin who was a fighter. In Puerto Rico, fighting is one way out of poverty." Tita smiled at Norm. "Education is another."

"You gotta have heart to be a fighter. White boys don't need the abuse these days, that's why your good boxers have been black or Hispanic for years." Norm steered a steady course back toward Key West. "The European fighters do well on the Continent, but when matched against an American black fighter, they lose badly. It's like, if you put an English guy up against an Irish Catholic from Northern Ireland, the Catholic's gonna probably win, because winning is more important to him. He has more to gain."

"I don't understand boxing," Tita said. "It's like something from the Romans and Christians."

"But the Christians don't die this time." Bob tossed his empty beer can into the rubbish bag.

"My cousin died in the ring," Tita said, and everyone was quiet.

"People die crossing the street, people minding their own business get shot every day. Dying is in all our futures." Norm smiled at her.

"I don't understand why people pay to see men beat each other. I didn't mean to make it an argument."

"No one is arguing." Norm continued to smile. "Maybe it's a small deformed gene in us, thousands of years old, from when we fought to survive. Or maybe, it's just blood lust."

Bob handed out fresh beer as a peace offering.

One of the cruise ships had left while we were out, but the other stood majestic against Key West's background as we sailed into the harbor. Burt rolled in the jib, while Bob and Tita prepared to take down the mainsail.

"Padre Thomas, I am glad you came along. I don't think this crew could have said a decent prayer." Norm started the engine.

"Thank you. There was so much more to say, but the words eluded me. I knew Tom, not as well as the others, but he was a friend. I fear that the men who killed him have not finished their rampage, and it frightens me." Thomas stared at me.

"It looks like we're due some weather," Bob pointed toward the north. "We should've checked before leaving."

"Cold front moving through, but that was supposed to be tonight," Thomas said.

"I think we can make the slip before the rain." Bob began tying off the mainsail.

Norm stared at the channel between Christmas Tree Island and Sunset Key and pointed, "Is that someone in the water?"

"Someone probably bathing." Burt finished with the roller furling. "A lot of homeless live on the island."

Norm gave the tiller to Tita and got the binoculars from the companionway. He focused on the person in the water.

"Can we get in there?" he said to Tita.

"Sure," and she changed course.

As we approached, we saw a person thrashing in the water. The current in the channel is notorious for its strength and speed.

"It's a woman," Norm said, amazed. "And she's in trouble."

"I'll get the dinghy." I stood up and looked toward the woman.

"Get it quick and meet me," Norm said, slipped off his deck shoes and shirt, handed me the binoculars, and dove into the water.

"Damn it!" Tita yelled, looking for Norm. "Where is he?"

"Off starboard!" I watched Norm swim against the current.

Bob tossed the life ring into the water and Norm grabbed it as he fought the current and swam toward the woman. If he had waited, the current would have brought her to him.

Tita steered away until she could see Norm, then she slowed the engine and the *Fenian Bastard* barely moved against the current. The GPS indicated we were not moving at all. The woman disappeared under the water and Norm dove, letting go of the life ring. It floated away, but Bob grabbed it with the pole hook as it passed the boat. There was no use getting the dinghy, time and the current were against Norm. Burt snatched another line from the rail and was prepared to toss it, if necessary.

When he surfaced, Norm had the frenzied woman under one

arm and the current swept them along. If we were not quick, the fast-moving water would take them out into the harbor's boat traffic. There was more to fear from tourists on Jet Skis than charter boats, once you entered the harbor. The water swirled around them, showing its force, trying to suck them down.

"Drop the ladder," I yelled.

Burt untied the line that kept the ladder folded and the top steps came undone and splashed into the water. Bob tied a line to the life ring, and was ready to toss it as soon as Norm got close. He tied the other end of the line onto the aft cleat, so if it pulled out of his hands because of the current and weight of two people, the line wouldn't be lost.

Norm and the panicky woman approached quickly, the force of the water pushing them, covering them at moments so they were submerged. We could see she was resisting his help; Norm held her and managed to swim toward the boat. As strong as he was, he couldn't keep this up much longer, especially with the woman and the current fighting him.

Bob moved forward with the life ring. He tossed it about ten feet ahead of Norm and the woman. The current pushed Norm toward it, but he was unable to grab on. The hysterical woman and Norm swiftly floated toward our stern. Bob pulled the life ring's line in. He prepared for another toss. He worked his way aft, waiting for the right opportunity.

At some point, Norm would have to let her go or they would both drown. The current was still sucking them along. Norm turned in the water to keep the woman from hitting the boat. His back whacked the aft section of the hull. We felt the forceful thud. Bob lowered the life ring a few feet in front of them. The current carried Norm to it and he grabbed the life ring with his free arm. Bob and Burt pulled the line, and Norm moved slowly toward the boat ladder. He held onto the woman as the current tried to take her away.

If this didn't work, they would pass us and be in the harbor before we could turn the boat. I took the line and let Bob, the youngest and tallest, climb down a few steps of the ladder, to help Norm.

We could hear the sobs of the woman as she pleaded to be let go.

Bob missed the life ring. Burt and I pulled Norm back toward the ladder, fighting the current.

"Got 'em!" Bob yelled.

Norm pushed the woman toward Bob, who grabbed her under her arms and lifted. She was naked. Burt tied the line to a second cleat and we wrestled the frightened woman from Bob and put her in the cockpit.

"Take the tiller." Tita ran below to get something to cover the woman. I took the tiller.

Burt helped Norm back aboard, and in the brief time Tita was gone it was impossible not to notice the bruises on the woman's body, her black eyes and raw-looking bruises on her wrists and ankles. She rolled up in the fetus position and screamed unrecognizable sounds.

"Those are cigarette burn marks on her breasts." Norm dripped water, and blood trickled from his back. "Someone tortured her."

We stared at the white, water-wrinkled, circular marks on her breasts.

Tita bent down and shooed us away, as she covered the woman with a large towel.

"You're all right," Tita said softly.

The woman looked up, saw Tita, and cried, "Don't hurt me."

I turned the boat back toward the channel and Garrison Bight.

"No one is going to hurt you. You're safe now. What happened?"

The woman looked around and saw us standing over her. She trembled.

"Let's go below and get you some clothes," Tita spoke softly.

"No!" she cried. "I'm not going below, I'm not going below."

"Okay, I'll get you some clothes."

The woman grabbed onto Tita as she began to stand up.

"No! Don't leave me with them." She glanced at us and then turned away.

"Okay, guys, move away."

I moved as far back as possible, but kept the tiller in my hand. Bob, Burt, Padre Thomas, and Norm moved toward the bow. The woman's gaze followed them and then turned to me.

"He has to steer the boat." Tita wrapped the towel around the woman and then helped her sit up. "I can go get you clothes, or you can come with me."

"I won't go below," she screamed. "Don't leave me."

"Norm, get one of my shirts and a pair of shorts from below for her." I stayed at the tiller and tried not to look at Tita and the woman.

Norm tossed a T-shirt and pair of shorts from the cabin, Tita grabbed them and helped the woman dress while we turned our backs.

Norm came out in a pair of dry shorts, and a towel over his shoulders covered the cuts on his back.

"Mick, I think it's time to clean the barnacles off the bottom." He used the towel as a large Band-Aid.

"This is Norm, the man who saved you," Tita said to the woman. "Wouldn't you like to say thank you?"

The woman stared at Norm and finally shook her head no. She looked like a rag mop with damp clothes and wet, unruly blonde hair.

"Do you want to tell me what happened?"

"I want my friends," the woman cried.

"What is your name?"

"Michelle. I need my friends."

"Where are they?"

"On that horrible boat," the woman sobbed. "Someone has to help them."

"Whose boat is it?"

"Three Cubans!" she continued to sob. "Horrible . . . men . . . horrible."

"They're not here, Michelle," Tita said. "We're going to help you and your friends."

"They kept us tied on the boat. They did horrible things to us." Michelle touched her breasts and cried. "I wanted to die."

"Is that why you were in the water?" Tita rubbed Michelle's head.

Michelle nodded.

"You're safe now, so you don't need to think about dying any longer."

Tita pulled Michelle to her and let her sob.

We were following the shoreline of Fleming Key. Bob took the tiller and I went below for my cell phone to call Richard. No one had said anything, but when Michelle said "three Cubans," we looked at each other in amazement.

SEVENTEEN

Norm came into the cabin as I talked with Richard Dowley on my cell phone, the towel hanging loosely over his shoulders. Most of the cuts on his back had clotted and the dried blood stuck to the towel.

"I'll make sure a woman officer meets you at the dock," Richard said, his voice drained. "An ambulance, too."

"Three Cubans," I said.

"Tell me about it at the dock." He disconnected, not wanting to argue.

I closed the cell phone and looked at Norm.

"You know I don't believe in coincidences." He leaned against the galley sink and pulled a T-shirt from his bag. "Three Cubans and three Cubans don't add up to six."

"Yeah," I exhaled a deep breath, "I think we all had that same thought."

"Bob said you have photos of two of them." Norm pulled the towel from around his shoulders and a few of the small cuts on his back began bleeding. He slipped the T-shirt on.

I lifted the chart tabletop, removed the small manila envelope that held Lu's photos and handed it to him.

"I don't want Bob and Burt involved, this isn't something they understand."

"They watch too many Bruce Willis movies?"

"Something like that."

"Reminds me of a young journalist I knew twenty years ago."

"Real funny, Norm. You and I know what we're dealing with. They haven't a clue," I said.

"Mick, if this stays local, we may need as many people on our side as we can get; especially if the cops ain't on our side." He flipped the envelope over.

"You did a good job out there," I wanted to change the subject. "Why?"

He looked at me with a confused expression and then a thin smile. "A damsel in distress, what else could I do?"

"You risked your life . . ."

"First," he cut me off, "I had no idea how strong that current was, and second, how often does anyone get to save a naked lady? And I thought you were coming in the dinghy." He pulled the photos from the envelope. "Only two?"

"Yeah, the third guy, Pepe, wasn't at the bar the second time."

"Maybe the guy in charge, gone to report in?" He looked at the photos. "I want to show these to Michelle, see if she recognizes them."

"Do you think she's ready for that?" I wondered if she could handle anything at the moment.

"She's gonna try to forget all this. That's what she'll try to do, and that's what all the shrinks will tell her she has to do, so now is the best time. She won't ever forget," he said, almost sadly. "How do you forget torture?"

"Why was she fighting you out there? You were trying to save her."

"She wanted to die," he said coldly. "Torture takes away your will to live and death can seem like a reward." He put the photos back in the envelope.

"Let Tita show them to her."

"Tita's not the right person for this, she's her friend right now, and she should remain that. I can be the heavy. I've done this before." Norm walked to the hatch and began to climb up toward the deck. "You comin'?"

"Hell, Norm, how'd it get to this?"

"You wanted to sail to Cuba," he turned to me, smiled and went on deck.

Bob was at the tiller and we were on the other side of Fleming Key, less than a half hour from the marina. The sunny afternoon sky had turned steel gray and getting darker as the *Fenian Bastard* motored through dark choppy water at five knots.

Tita leaned against the bulkhead and held Michelle. She spoke softly to the distraught woman and stroked her head. Burt and Padre Thomas had attached the canvas flap that fit between the Bimini and dodger so it would keep the cockpit dry in a light rain. The darkening sky promised more.

Norm sat across from Tita and waited for her to look at him. The weather began to worsen and the *Fenian Bastard* tossed lightly against small windswept waves. Burt and Padre Thomas sat under the Bimini, as far away from Tita as they could.

"Tita, I need Michelle to look at these photos," Norm held out the brown envelope and spoke softly, his words almost lost in the wind. "It's important and it may help us find the men who did this to her."

Michelle lifted her head, as Tita shook her head no. Norm removed one photo from the envelope.

"Michelle," Norm spoke slowly and clearly to the nervous woman. "We're returning from spreading the ashes of a friend who was killed by three Cubans. We need to know if they are the same men that kidnapped you and your friends."

Michelle showed no sign of understanding. She curled up closer to Tita, her arms folded tightly across her chest.

"Don't you want to help your friends?" Norm stood and moved a step closer. Michelle cringed and Tita gave him a hard stare, challenging his right to talk to the victim like that. "In an hour the police will be showing you these photos and asking you questions. If you wait an hour, it's another hour your friends are on that boat. Don't you think the men are angry that you escaped?" Norm's voice had lost its caring tone. "Won't they take that anger out on your friends, hurt them because you're gone?" He moved a step closer. "Don't you want to help them? Michelle's safe now, so she doesn't care. Is that it?"

"Norm," Tita snapped.

"I pulled her out of the water, Tita. I saved her life and we both almost drowned," he said harshly. "She wanted to die, she wanted to save her friends, I heard it all from her and now she has a chance to help them and she's hiding behind you."

Norm's words were cruel. They had to be, to break through a barrier of self-hatred Michelle was feeling as a survivor. She had wanted to die and didn't, and now she was safe, but her friends were still in their private hell. She felt relieved, and hated herself for it. Norm's use of cruelty against self-pity had helped put my life back together after the bombing in Tijuana. I hated him while he was doing it, but I eventually understood why he needed to do what he did, and I got on with my life. The nightmares were still there, but I dealt with them.

Michelle gave Norm a blank stare as she unwrapped one arm and reached out to him. He handed her a photo. She held it at arm's length, afraid it could hurt her if it got any closer, and stared at it. She began to cry and opened her hand quickly, as if the photo was on fire, and let it fall to the deck, slowly nodding her head.

Norm picked up the photo. "Michelle, are these the men?"

She pulled her head from Tita's shoulder and looked at him. She nodded, again.

"Tell me, don't nod. Yes or no?" He stood over her.

Tears streamed down her cheeks when she said, "Yes, it's them."

I sat across the cockpit from Tita and read Michelle's lips, but she spoke so softly I could not hear her.

"Thank you," Norm's voice was friendly again. "You have helped your friends." He put the photo back in the envelope and handed it to me.

The first rain began to fall. It came down slowly, but the wind blew it into the cockpit and we were getting wet. I took the tiller and Burt, Bob, and Padre Thomas went below, out of the weather. Tita tried to get Michelle to go below but she refused. Norm stood next to me.

At the marina's parking lot red flashing lights from a city ambulance reflected off the boats, the repetitious glow made more ominous by the rain. Some of the forms at the slip wore yellow slickers; others had blue KWPD windbreakers on. I was too far away to pick out Richard, but I knew he was there.

"You know these guys are crazy," Norm's words were almost lost in the wind. "If you don't kill them, they'll kill you."

EIGHTEEN

The rain was light, but it blew everywhere, and the wind made docking the *Fenian Bastard* tricky. Bob, Burt, and Padre Thomas came out of the cabin, accepting their fate. Bob and Burt knew what to do. They grabbed pole hooks and moved to the bow to catch the pull-line running between the slip's two starboard pilings and the dock. As soon as the bow crossed the outer piling, I put the engine in neutral. The wind began to push the *Fenian Bastard* toward the pilings.

"Got it," Bob yelled.

I snapped the engine into reverse to keep the boat from moving forward too fast, and when I saw Burt had caught the line, too, I went back into neutral. Bob grabbed the line by hand and Burt put the pole hook away and threw a bowline to someone on the dock. Norm jumped onto the finger dock with a stern line and pulled the boat up against the rubber fenders. Burt tossed the spring line to Norm, who pulled it to the finger dock's aft cleat and tied it tight. I shut the engine off.

Richard Dowley and Luis Morales were on the dock wearing their KWPD windbreakers and baseball hats pulled down tight. Four other cops were there in yellow slickers, and two paramedics stood by a gurney. Everyone was wet and the sky was getting darker and more threatening.

Michelle was afraid to get off the boat, no matter what Tita said to her. We left them aboard and joined the police.

"She's afraid to come down," I told Richard. "Where's the

woman cop?"

He waved over someone in a slicker.

"Officer Patti Bolter," he introduced her.

"We've got a problem, Patti." I told her and Richard what had happened.

When the others realized what we were talking about, they crowded around and listened. Sometimes they glanced toward the boat, the wet expressions on their faces showing disbelief. Saving a naked woman from drowning was unusual, even in Key West, but a naked tortured woman was something else all together.

"Patti, maybe you can help Tita convince Michelle to come off the boat." Lightning flashed as I spoke and, within seconds, a thunderous boom exploded over us.

"I can do that and I'll go with her to the hospital." She took off her slicker, gave it to one of the officers, and climbed aboard in her blue police uniform. She knew that a woman in a police uniform would offer Michelle some reassurance.

"The crisis people are waiting at the hospital," Richard said. "Maybe I should have had them here."

"You need to find that boat. It may already be too late," I said.

"She didn't say anything descriptive about the boat?"

"Nothing."

"The Coast Guard has two small boats out, but they don't know what they're looking for. I told them to look for anyone that seemed out of place or in a hurry. I promised Executive Officer Fitton I'd call back with more information."

Patti stood up at the rail. "If you all move back to the parking lot, she'll come down."

Richard gave the hand signal and everyone moved away. The paramedics shut off the ambulance's flashing light and the eerie feeling disappeared. The dock became surreal in the rain.

Headlights from cars traveling too fast along North Roosevelt Boulevard persistently splashed their glow through the rain and across the water to the dock. The paramedics put the gurney back into the ambulance.

Tita and Patti walked with Michelle between them. Michelle seemed drawn in on herself and looked much smaller than the other women. Tita couldn't have been five-six, Patti not much taller, but Michelle looked like a child as they walked along the dock.

Detective Morales was talking to Bob, Burt, and Padre Thomas. Norm stayed close to me.

"Richard, she identified the two Cubans in the photo," I said.

"If everything you've said happened to this woman, how can you believe her, Mick?" he wiped the rain from his face with his damp hand. "She has to be going out of her mind." Richard seemed to notice Norm for the first time.

"You won't check it out?"

"Yeah, I'll talk to her, but it won't be tonight. The crisis people and doctors will get her first."

"Someone has to ask her about the boat, get some details."

"The crisis team, Mick, they'll do what's best for her, it's what they do."

The rain became heavy as the sky darkened and the wind gusts picked up. I was soaked to the bone and everyone else was, too. It was late afternoon, but winter darkness had settled in early. This was a storm coming through, not an afternoon tropical shower.

"Have we met?" Richard turned to Norm.

Norm stuck his arm out to shake hands. "No, we haven't. I'm Norm Burke."

"And where to do you fit into all this, Norm?" They shook hands.

"Mick and I go way back."

"Before he moved to Key West?"

"Oh yeah, way back."

"We'll have to spend some time discussing him. He always been . . ."

"A pain in the ass?" Norm cut Richard off.

"I was looking for something more polite, but yeah, a pain in the ass will do."

"Always," Norm said.

The paramedics climbed out of the ambulance as the women approached. The women stopped at the edge of the mangroves and Tita came forward.

"She's nervous because there are so many men here," she said to Richard.

"We're cops."

"How can she tell?" Tita glanced at the officers in yellow rain gear. "Stenciled letters on the back don't mean anything to her, right now."

"What can we do, Tita?"

"Let Patti take her to the hospital in a police car," she pushed a clump of wet hair out of her face. "Make sure they have a woman doctor at the emergency room. She'll freak if it's a man who tries to treat her."

Richard walked over to the paramedics, said something we couldn't hear, and then had one of the officers drive a police car close to the ambulance. He got out and left the engine running.

"We're going to follow you, Tita," Richard said.

"I'll sit with her in back, Patti will drive and she'll drive slow, no flashing lights or sirens."

"We'll follow you quietly."

Tita went over to Michelle and Patti and the three walked slowly to the waiting police car. Michelle walked like someone facing the impossible and in no hurry to get there. Tita and

Patti supported her by the arms the whole way. They got in the car and drove off. The ambulance left right behind them.

"Mick, the rest of you go to the police station and give Morales your statements," Richard said.

"I'm securing the boat and then we'll go over."

"Tell Morales." He got into his unmarked car and sped off.

"You want me to wait?" Morales said.

"Luis, I'm gonna lock up and check the lines, there's nothing else that can be done in this weather. We'll meet you at the station in fifteen minutes."

"Don't be late." He got into his police car and drove off, windshield wipers twitching on high.

Norm and I locked up the *Fenian Bastard* and made sure the lines were tight.

The interior of my Jeep was soaked, but it was beyond mattering at that point, so we packed in. We couldn't have gotten any wetter if we walked the two blocks. A red light at Palm Avenue and North Roosevelt made us stop, so we waited to turn right. Traffic rushed along the half-flooded boulevard. It took us less than five minutes to get there.

"Do we mention Tom?" Burt said as we stood in the outdoor hallway.

"No," I said. "We were sailing to sail, and just tell what actually happened as we were heading in, nothing else. No need to mention Tom or our suspicions about the Cubans."

"What suspicions?" Padre Thomas winked at me.

We looked like drowned rats. I picked up the outdoor phone and asked dispatch for Detective Morales.

"Mick, Morales knows about the Cubans," Bob said. "We mentioned it to him at the marina."

"Shit!"

"We thought everyone knew," Burt said.

"They do now," I said.

Luis, dressed casually, dry, every hair in place, and two officers in uniforms, met us at the door and gave us towels. We dried off as best as we could in the hallway and followed them to a small conference room on the second floor.

"Put the towels on the chair before you sit down," Luis said.

After we sat, Luis read a statement about what had happened and how we came upon Michelle and what she said to us. He had quickly put it together from talking to Bob, Burt, and Padre Thomas at the dock. There was no mention of *gusanos* or Tom's ashes.

"Is this right?" he asked.

We nodded or said yes.

"Nothing more to add?"

We said nothing.

"An officer will bring in a copy of this. Read it, and if you agree with it as your statement, please sign it," he said. "Mick, can I see you outside?" He stood and left the room.

I followed him outside and down the hallway to a small kitchen that had a patio where officers smoked. We went in, I could see the rain pouring from the black sky, and I could hear it beating on the patio.

"Gusanos," Luis said angrily. "You withheld evidence from me about Tom. Why?"

"When you came to the sail club I didn't know anything." His anger caught me off guard. "It was a few days later that I heard the rumor about the three Cubans, and Tom was still alive."

"And when did you get the photos? When were you going to share them?" Bob and Burt hadn't realized how little Luis knew when he questioned them on the dock. Luis walked to the patio door and looked out, his back to me.

"It had to be a week after all this happened."

"And you didn't think to share?" He turned. "It's evidence,

116

Mick. You guys looking for these Cubans on your own? You vigilantes now, taking justice into your own hands?" He sat at the kitchen table. "You don't think I'll do my job?"

I stared out the window, watching the rainfall, before I said anything. Richard had thrown me to the wolves with the two feds, so I decided there was no need to take grief from Luis because of him. It wasn't an easy decision, but I was more concerned with covering my ass than I was about covering Richard's.

"I'm not a vigilante and I didn't withhold evidence. As soon as I received the photos, I called the Chief and gave him copies."

Luis looked at me with a surprised expression, questioning my comment. I could tell he didn't believe me, but then his expression changed and I knew he did.

"The Chief knew about this, he had copies of the photos?" He looked me square in the eyes, wanting me to flinch.

"Yeah, and he ran the names we had for them."

"And what came back?" His expression continued to darken, like the clouds outside.

"Two federal assholes, calling themselves Smith and Jones."

"You've lost me."

"Federal agents called the Chief to find out why he was running the two names . . ."

"I thought there were three?" he cut me off.

"Only had photos of two, with names, but we weren't sure the names were real."

"Okay, go on."

"The Chief gave them the info on Tom and a couple of days later they came here to interview me."

Luis stood and looked out the window, again. "Why wasn't I told?" I didn't answer because he wasn't talking to me. "Does the Chief still have the photos?"

"I have no idea."

"It's my case." He stared out the window. "What did you tell the Feds?"

"Nothin'. They told me."

Luis turned. "You're losing me again."

"Luis, I am going to tell you briefly what happened and if you want to know more, talk to the Chief, he was there." He nodded unhappily. "They told me the three men were their agents, and at the time of Tom's beating they were in Miami for a wedding. They couldn't have been involved, because they couldn't have been in Key West."

"What about the photos?"

"Wrong guys, they said."

"But the Cubans are working with them, right?"

"Right. And, I don't believe them. They'd say anything to protect these three guys."

"You're not telling me something, Mick."

"Anything else has to come from the Chief."

"Goddamn it! This is my case." He gave me a long second to answer him and then he walked out of the kitchen, punching numbers into his cell phone.

Tita was alone in the conference room when I returned.

"Where'd they go?"

"To PT's for something to eat," she said. "They want us to meet them, but I need to change."

"Are you hungry?"

"Exhausted, I can't be hungry."

"Me, too. You want to come to the boat and take a shower and clean up?"

"Thanks. I don't want to be alone."

I didn't ask her what happened at the hospital, but I wanted to.

NINETEEN

The sky appeared darker, the rain got heavier, and the wind gusts stronger, as Tita and I left the police station.

"I want a shower, Mick, let's just go." She walked into the rain, reminding me of Luis at the sail club, walking as if the rain didn't exist.

"If we had a bar of soap right now."

"I want a hot shower." She got into the Jeep's front seat. "A long, hot shower and then I want to sleep for a week."

I made a left on Roosevelt, a right on Eisenhower, and another right on Palm Avenue. It was the long way around, but a *No Left Turn* sign at Roosevelt and Palm didn't leave many choices. At the bottom of the Palm Avenue Bridge, where Eisenhower and Palm meet, the road was flooded. Heavy rain always flooded the area. The end-of-day, rush-hour traffic still inched its way along, even though it was past six. Weather and accidents are the common causes of rush-hour delays in Key West. We waited at the stop sign until someone felt sorry for the two soaked people in a Jeep and waved us in front of them. I flashed my lights in thanks and Tita waved.

Off in the distance we heard thunder, but didn't see any lightning. Tita was quiet and the radio had US1 104.1FM playing, but it was hard to hear. We had missed newsman Bill Becker's six o'clock news. Bill, with more than twenty-five years of news experience in the Keys, has his finger on the pulse of Key West, and I wondered if someone from the marina or the police had given him a heads-up on Michelle. He had called me within an hour of my leaving Richard's house on the Saturday I found Tom, and he's off Saturdays. Everyone in the Lower Keys calls Bill with news tips, accident reports and everyone in the Lower Keys listens to Bill for that reason.

Turning left into the marina was easy, after we drove over the bridge and down the only hill in Key West. Tita got out of the Jeep and walked through the rain and wind, determined to get her hot shower. I was right behind her.

While I unlocked the main cabin hatch Tita stood next to me and I caught her staring at the section in the cockpit where she had held Michelle and tried to comfort the hysterical woman for more than an hour. I could almost see the event replaying in her head. Rain was blowing into the cockpit, so I couldn't tell if tears or rain covered her cheeks.

Tita went right to the bow cabin and closed the door. The head and shower were accessible from the cabin.

"I need some dry clothes," I said.

She tossed me a pair of shorts and a T-shirt and closed the door. Rain pounded the deck, its cadence music to my ears. The explosions of thunder, softened by distance, accented the rhapsody. I tossed my wet clothes out on deck, toweled off, and dressed. The air-conditioning hummed quietly and it brought fresh air into the cabin. I took Tom Corcoran's latest book, *Air Dance Iguana,* and picked up reading where I'd left off. You needed to live in Key West as long as Tom had to capture the island's life the way he does.

There is no such thing as privacy when you live on a boat. The main cabin had an entrance to the head and I heard the shower start. The small water heater could offer a short burst of hot, hot water or about five minutes of lukewarm water.

The *Fenian Bastard* rocked in her berth. It was a motion that often helped me to sleep at night. When I finished two chapters of Tom's book I thought Tita would be out of the shower, because I knew the warm water was gone. I went to the head's door and listened. The shower was still on and as I got closer, I could hear her crying.

I stepped back a little. "You okay? That water can't be too hot now." I didn't want her to think I was eavesdropping, or to know I heard her crying.

"A few more minutes, Mick."

"You hungry?"

"Tired. Can we take a nap?"

"Sure, but you need to come out of the shower first."

"A couple of more minutes," she said.

I finished three more chapters of Tom's book before the shower shut off. I heard her searching through the cabin for clothes. She walked into the main cabin in loose shorts and a green Hog's Breath T-shirt that was too large.

"How do I look?" She turned like a model.

"Clean and beautiful," I said, and put the book down.

Her long black hair was damp and combed straight back and she smelled of soap and shampoo. A redness remained around her green eyes, but she looked more relaxed. Maybe she cried herself that way. She hugged me tighter than she ever had.

"A one-hour nap and then we can go to PT's and eat," she whispered into my ear. "Okay?" The hug ended and she held my hand.

"I have food here, we don't have to go anywhere."

"I don't know if I can sleep with the noise and rocking." She led me toward the aft cabin. "I want to sleep in the small bed. Give me an hour and then we'll decide."

The aft cabin's bed is big enough for two, but not as comfortable as the bow cabin's. Dim light filtered through the portholes. She fluffed the two pillows and we lay down on top of the comforter. Tita hugged my right arm and snuggled her head next to my shoulder. The rain beat a rhythm on the deck and the wind rocked the boat. We lay quietly for a while and I could feel her small attempts to find a comfortable spot. I wasn't sure she would find it next to me.

Maybe she needed to cry some more, I thought, and realized that the three Cubans had affected a lot of us without our knowing them; their crimes had many victims besides Tom and Michelle and her friends. Tita was a victim. Even Norm had become a victim when he chose to save the damsel in distress. I realized the responsibility of the crimes rested on others as well. There were Smith and Jones—whose side was Richard on?—and who else in Washington knew of this plan to topple the Cuban communist government, and how many in Cuba knew? To whom was this plan so important that the lives of innocent people didn't matter? The list grew as the clock ticked.

"Why?" she said softly, but I didn't answer. "How could a person do what they did to Michelle? This is something out of a horror movie." Her voice reflected her weariness.

"I wish I had an answer for you," I said. "I don't."

"I wonder if there is an answer." She kissed my hand. "Norm knew she'd been tortured with just one quick look."

"In his line of work he's probably dealt with torture victims before."

"Is he a good guy? He seems like a good guy—I like him—or is there another side of the coin?" She placed her arm across my chest. "Would you tell me if you knew?"

"I know Norm's my friend and I know he's been an agent for a federal agency, probably one we've never heard of, without initials. He's tough, and sometimes that makes him cruel."

"Like when he made Michelle identify the photo?"

"Yeah, like that." I hadn't told Tita about Tijuana and how Norm had pulled me out of my blackness. I wasn't ready to tell her. "But I'm not sure you can call what he did cruel, not in comparison, when you consider what the *gusanos* did to her."

"I think he did what he did to help find Tom's killer and maybe find the men who hurt Michelle," she said quietly. "It wasn't about him, maybe that's the difference."

"Maybe," I said.

"You didn't ask me what happened at the hospital."

"I know you'll tell me, eventually."

She was quiet for a minute and her arm pulled tighter across my chest.

"Patti and the two crisis counselors stayed with her," Tita sounded exhausted. "They told me to leave. Richard was there. She looked frightened when I left and I felt like I was deserting her."

"You helped save her."

"You think so?"

"If you hadn't been with us, we couldn't have handled her without force, and she didn't need that."

The rain beat down, the boat continued to rock, and finally her arm lightened, and I knew she was asleep. She would have dreams, nightmares, for a long time. In some of them, she would probably see herself in Michelle's place. I knew the feeling. The nightmares would take on a life of their own, forcing her to see things that hadn't happened, but they would come to life and seem real, if only for a few minutes in her head. She would wake up terrified, and even knowing it was only a dream, she would not feel safe. Going to bed, to sleep, would become a challenge. Her mind would play tricks on her and it was going to be difficult to separate reality from imagination. There was nothing I could do but try to be there for her.

I wondered if Michelle would have anyone to be there for her.

When I woke, the rain was no longer playing its tune against the cabin. I listened to the quiet and felt the *Fenian Bastard* gently rock. Tita was rolled up next to me, hugging herself. I wondered where she was, maybe back in Boston, safe in her bed at Paco's house or back in Puerto Rico, a little girl riding a horse in the hills of Lares. I hoped she was in one of those places.

I envy people who can lie in bed after waking up, because I can't. I've known some who will spend Sunday morning in bed reading the paper. When I wake up, I get out of bed and begin my day.

I stared at the porthole and it was still dark outside. Carefully, I moved off the bed and walked into the main cabin, leaving the door open so I could hear her. It was ten o'clock. When I opened the hatch the night sky was clearing, and the rain had stopped. Off in the distance lightning flashed and filled the clouds with bright, broken images. Cars sped along North Roosevelt. The wind splashed small swells against the hull. I checked my cell phone on the chart table, I had no calls. Why hadn't Norm called? They couldn't be at PT's this long.

I heard the soft drone of a boat engine and figured someone was heading out to their mooring, now that the weather had moved off. I turned on the light over the settee, picked up Tom's book, and began reading. But, I was hungry, so I took some cottage cheese out of the frig, mixed in fruit and ate. Cottage cheese and beer, what a diet this day had given me. I was hungry and the image of the cheeseburger at PT's popped into my head. I finished the cottage cheese.

I went back to reading and after a few chapters I looked up and Tita was in the doorway. She smiled but couldn't pull it off, she was still worn out.

"Go back to sleep." I put the book down.

"Something's going on outside," she said.

I got up, slid open the hatch and stuck my head out.

The forty-six-foot yawl at the end of the T-dock was swathed in flames. The fire department's boat was coming through the cut at Hilton Haven, its red lights flashing, and I heard sirens from the street.

TWENTY

Fingers of flames crawled up the main and the mizzenmasts. The red-yellow blaze slurped across both booms on the wooden yawl, eating the wrapped sails while its flickering brightness encircled the dock and black water. A shimmering inferno engulfed the deck.

Traffic along North Roosevelt slowed to watch the spectacle.

"A boat fire." I rushed on deck.

The T-dock was only three slips away, but the wind was blowing toward the boulevard, away from the *Fenian Bastard*. The other good news was that the fireboat was already spreading water against the flames, its generator pulsing loudly, helping the pump force saltwater through the hose and onto the fire. Five firefighters ran down the dock, two stopped and each opened an emergency fire-hose box. They pulled the hoses, which worked off city waterlines, toward the burning boat.

"Can we do anything?" Tita stared at the hypnotic flames.

I hadn't heard her come up on deck. Excitement and noise started to waken the live-aboard residents. If they weren't at a dock party or out on the town, live aboards were an early-to-bed group. A boat fire would frighten them all out onto the dock.

"The wind's on our side," I pointed to the flames that blew toward the boulevard, where cars stopped at the curb and spectators watched from the seawall. The stench from the smoke began to engulf the dock.

The Key West Fire Department's normal response time is three minutes. There are three fire stations on the island. The main emergency complex stood next to the police station, and kept its fireboat in a slip across the street in the bay. After this call had come in, all the firefighters on the boat had to do was go under the Palm Avenue Bridge to reach the burning boat.

We could feel the heat from the flames. I watched for hot ashes that could twist in the wind, land on my sails and burn small holes. I hadn't put on the sail covers earlier, so I was concerned. Luckily, it had rained heavily.

"I've never seen a boat fire before." Tita held my hand. "It's incredible, but . . ."

The owners of the boat lived in Northern Michigan, snow-birds that usually arrived the first of January and sailed around the Caribbean until late April or early May and then returned to the woods. The week or so they spent at the marina, supplying the boat, checking for needed repairs, they were friendly and we shared a drink or two at the dock and at Finnegan's Wake, the couple's favorite local watering hole. Before they returned north, they spent another week at the marina to winterize the boat. Their names were Judy and Joe Hart, but I had no idea what they did the rest of the year. I knew they had their boat work done at a small marina on the south side of Cuba, because they had given me a business card for the place and recommended it. We also enjoyed corned beef and cabbage at Finnegan's together.

"Who was on the boat?" Tita asked.

"A couple of snowbirds own it, but I haven't seen them."

"Could a fire start without them being onboard?"

"An electrical fire could."

The masts and booms sizzled as the water hit, but slowly they stopped burning and the water was directed toward the deck. At first the deck flames subsided, but as the firefighters stood by patiently, the flames shot up midship and smoke ballooned into the night.

Fire Marshall Paul Fraga called my name from the dock. He was dressed in civvies. "Mick, it couldn't get much closer, could it?"

I climbed down to meet him on the dock.

"Close enough for me." We shook hands.

"Anyone on the boat?"

"Not unless they came in while I was out. Snowbirds."

"You haven't seen any homeless hanging on the docks?"

"Too many residents around for strangers to go unnoticed."

I turned to see Tita standing in the shadows. Paul and I watched the firefighters spray more water on the burning boat.

"How long before we sink it?"

"I don't know. If it's electrical the bilge pumps aren't working, so it shouldn't be too much longer."

"If it's not electrical?"

"What else could it be?"

"Come on." We moved to the end of the pier. "Stay here." Paul talked to one of the firemen using the hose.

He spoke into a radio and all the hoses stopped spraying. Paul waved me over.

"Watch," he said.

In a moment, the fire returned.

"Propane," he said to the firefighter and me. "Propane leak," he said into the handheld radio. "Someone was onboard, propane doesn't turn itself on."

The fireboat backed off and stopped directing water onto the smoldering yawl and one of the crews on the fire hoses stopped, too, the other hose crew directed water to where the flames were coming from.

"Can it explode?" I was concerned.

"No, the water will cool the propane tank and one of the

guys will turn it off."

Fire Chief Billy Fahey joined us. A boat fire brings everyone out, no matter the day or hour.

"It's over?" he said.

"Propane." The one word from Paul explained a lot to Billy.

"Who's going in?"

"You want to?"

"Right behind you, Paul."

Paul walked over to one of the firefighters and they discussed going in to shut off the propane tank.

"Is it a dirty job, Billy?" I asked.

"I think we've poured a lot of water into the cabin, so it's probably flooded. Whoever goes in is going to get wet, dirty depends on the condition of the cabin."

"The bilge pumps could've been working, maybe at first."

"We've got big pumps in the truck that will keep it from sinking."

"Julio's going in to shut it down. I think the tank has cooled off." Paul came over to us. "He likes doing this stuff, go figure. Vega will back him up."

"Will we need the pump?" Billy asked.

"I've radioed the truck, it's coming."

A police officer helped roll the large pump down from the fire truck. Live-aboard residents were out now and the police kept them back. Tita walked down to me.

"Are we okay to be this close?"

"We're safe, someone's going in to shut off the propane," I said.

"How did it start, if it's propane?"

"A good question," Billy said.

The hose crew turned the water hose off.

We watched Julio Avael in his heavy protective clothing climb onboard. The fireboat stood by, its hose pumping water back into the bight and the hose crews prepared to start pouring water back on the boat if the situation required it. Jerry Vega walked behind Julio. Though Billy and Paul made it seem that turning off the propane tank was routine, when it came to fire these men never accepted anything as routine. Routine cost lives in their profession.

No one could tell what condition the deck was in because of the fire, and if the firefighters moved too quickly, there could be a serious accident if the deck gave way. The men had high-powered flashlights and we watched them slowly search the area.

"The deck is no good," a voice crackled from a radio.

"Be careful. See if you can locate the propane canister," Billy spoke into the radio. "If it's not on deck, look for a kitchen area below."

"It's a mess," Julio's voice came from the radio. "No tank on deck. The cabin's flooded. I see some steps, I'm going to check them out and maybe go in."

"Carefully," Billy and Paul echoed each other into their radios.

"I'm in. We'll need the pump." The words screeched from the radio. "Damn, there are two tanks in the main cabin. I'm shutting them off."

Billy and Paul looked at me.

"That doesn't sound good," Paul said. "Why two tanks in the cabin? No one stores propane in a boat. Mick, will it sink?"

"It's low in the water." I checked the waterline. "What's the problem if you use the big pump?"

"It could pump out evidence of arson," Paul said. "But if it sinks, it's worse."

"Oh fuck," came from the radio.

"Julio, what's wrong?" Billy spoke into the radio, his voice anxious. "What's wrong?"

"Fuck it, damn it, Billy," came back from the radio, "there

130

are two bodies in here."

"Yeah, Mick," Billy turned to me, "it's gonna be a dirty job."

TWENTY-ONE

A police officer, assigned to the end of the T-dock to keep people away from a crime scene, moved the snooping live-aboard residents back to their boats. Another cop kept the curious out of the parking lot. From three slips away, Tita and I sat on the deck of the *Fenian Bastard* and watched the firefighters and police mingle as they set up lights to illuminate the yawl. A large generator hummed loudly. Lightning flashed off in the distance, the storm was moving away and stars began to show in the evening sky. The yawl sent small puffs of smoke into the night and the pungent order of burnt wood eddied through the marina. The wind blew toward the boulevard, taking most of the stench of death with it. To Tita it was just an unpleasant odor.

"What do you have to eat?" Tita yawned. "I think I'm hungry."

"You think you're hungry, you're not sure?"

"Okay, I'm hungry. I haven't eaten all day."

"Check the frig, I don't know what Norm left, but you should find some sandwich meats, cottage cheese and fruit."

Tita went below to check on food availability.

"It hasn't sunk yet," Paul Fraga called as he walked by wearing the protective clothing of the other firefighters. When the police detectives arrived, Paul would go into the burned-out cabin with them, checking for signs of arson. After the cops finished their preliminary investigation, the paramedics would remove the bodies and take them to the local morgue.

132

He stopped and walked to me.

"Billy's back at the station, trying to come up with some kind of screening that will catch anything pumped out from our hose." Even though it was cool, Paul looked hot. "He ask you about the people who own the boat?"

"Yeah, a couple from Michigan, but I haven't seen them."

"Well, if they came here to die, maybe they didn't want to be seen."

"That what the two propane tanks suggests, suicide?"

"Be my first guess, then arson."

"Arson and bodies . . ." I didn't finish my thought.

"Yeah, murder, maybe murder-suicide. Good luck trying to get some sleep tonight." He walked toward the yawl.

Tita brought two sandwiches and beers on deck and gave me one.

"Ham and pepper cheese," she said as she bit into her sandwich. "No chips, what kind of junk-food junkie are you?"

"The healthy kind. Where are the sweet pickles?"

She wrinkled her nose. "No pickles."

We watched the activities on the dock as we ate and drank our beers without talking. Tita took the plates below when we finished.

"Are you coming to bed?" she said from the hatchway. "It's after one already."

"I was hoping Richard would turn up with the detectives."

"I didn't think you were talking to him."

"I need to, but I won't wait much longer. When Paul goes aboard, it means all the cops are here."

"Wait a minute," Tita came back on deck. "Why are you waiting for Richard?"

I pulled her toward me, hugged her, but she pulled away.

"Does this involve the Cubans?" She waved her arm around and pointed toward the burned yawl. "Mick, don't keep things

133

from me, I'm part of this now."

"Wednesday night, on my way to the Hog's Breath, there was a Cuban guy standing by the mangroves in the parking lot." I turned to her and we sat down. The world was circling on me, because I didn't want her involved; I didn't want this to hurt her any more than it had already. "He bullshitted me with a story about wanting a slip, but he was checking me out. He asked me which boat was mine and I pointed to the yawl."

"Could they have burned up in it?" She said after a minute of silence. "Maybe they were waiting inside for you and something went wrong?"

I didn't tell her these guys were thorough and didn't make too many mistakes, at least not while they were together. And, I wondered about Smith's and Jones' involvement.

"Let's hope so," I said.

"What else could it be? You don't think it's the couple from Michigan, do you?"

"No, they're too noticeable when they come."

"Did you tell anyone about the Cuban?"

"Bob, Burt, and you."

"When will they identify the bodies?"

"It'll take a while, my guess is they're badly burned, so they might need dental records to ID 'em."

"That's sickening," she held her hand over her mouth. "I hope it's them and not some innocent people."

"Me, too." I feared if I told her what I really thought she would lose it. "Let's go to bed. Paul said sleeping was going to be difficult because of the noise they'll make when the pump-out starts and the lights go on."

"I could sleep through a hurricane." She forced a smile and we went below.

I played Bob Dylan CDs on the stereo and turned the sound down low. It was the music she heard her brother and me listen to years ago in Boston and I hoped it would mask the sounds to come from outside. I wanted it to help remind her of the past, so she could put today away and sleep without nightmares. I lit a citrus-scented candle in the galley to overcome the burnt smell that had crept into the main cabin. Somewhere before the first CD changed, we fell asleep.

My cell phone chirped a little after seven. I was alone in the aft cabin bed. I heard Tita answer it and got up.

"It's Norm," she handed me the phone.

"Yeah," I forced the sleep away.

"I hope I didn't interrupt anything."

"Where are you?" He didn't answer. "You hear about the fire on the dock last night?"

"I am at the Pier House. I took a small suite for us," there was no sleepiness in his voice. "Pack a bag and come over."

"There a reason for this?"

"Yeah, I'm trying to keep you alive. Room 408," he hung up.

"A reason for what?" Tita was in her outfit from yesterday. It was dry, but wrinkled.

"Norm wants me to stay with him at the Pier House."

"He knows how to treat himself."

I went on deck, the yellow police tape was up at the T-dock, and two policemen I didn't recognize stood guard. The burnt smell hung in the air.

"Do you think the bodies are still there?" Tita asked from the hatchway.

"No." I went below and tossed some jeans, Tommy Bahama shirts and T-shirts into my large West Marine duffle bag. "The paramedics took them last night."

Listening to Norm's advice had saved me before, maybe he had found out something. From its hiding place, I took the box that contained the Glock and extra clips and put it in the bag, along with some toiletries.

"I didn't hear an ambulance last night."

"They weren't in a hurry."

"You can stay with me," Tita handed me a cup of coffee.

"Let's go see Norm and find out what he has in mind, first."

"I need to shower and change. Come home with me?"

"I'll follow you."

She smiled honestly, her green eyes bright, as we finished our coffee. She was still afraid to be alone.

Norm's small suite contained three rooms, a living room with a large-screen TV, dinning table, two overstuffed chairs, and a sofa, and two bedrooms—one off each side of the living room—with king-size beds, TVs, and bathrooms. The view from the patio included the pool and the harbor.

Tita had changed into beige shorts and a mustard-colored T-shirt from the Songwriters' Festival at the Hog's Breath. She wore old tennis shoes without socks and her hair was pulled back into a long ponytail that swayed as she walked.

"Welcome," Norm greeted us at the door. His baggy shirt told me he had his gun holstered at his back. "Your room," he pointed to his left.

"Nice layout," Tita looked around. "I thought you were only staying a day or two."

"Things change," he said.

She went to check out his bedroom.

"We need to talk," he watched Tita walk into his room.

"She's not going away. I don't know what to do with her."

"I bet you didn't have that problem last night."

I ignored him and sat in one of the chairs.

"How'd you end up here?"

"Burt recommended it."

"How much is this costing?"

He laughed softly. "I'm using the company credit card."

"The company you don't work for?"

"Yeah, I figured it's the least they can do for us."

Confronted, he would deny any connection to a government agency, but he had no problem alluding to it. It was a game we've played for more than twenty years and most times, I enjoyed it.

I got up and tossed my bag on the bed in my room. Tita stood in the doorway.

"If you take a shower here, I promise not to rape you."

I wanted to get to the hotel in a hurry, so I let her shower alone at home.

"Thank you," I bowed and took my bag into the bathroom and locked the door.

Sleep and a hot shower can do wonders for a person. I dressed in a pair of old jeans, a loose Tommy Bahama shirt and fitted the Glock inside my pants, in back. I slipped on a pair of worn boat shoes. Two full clips went into my back pocket.

Tita and Norm were drinking coffee on the patio. Half a pot sat on the inside table. I poured myself a cup, added two sugars, and joined them.

"You get a tour of Duval Street last night?"

"Kind of." He stared at Tita and then continued, "We went barhopping, but couldn't find the Cubans. I met Lu and a couple of other strange characters. In fact, the later it got, the stranger they became."

"That happens in this town," I said.

"Tita, I have to talk to Mick."

"I'm not going anywhere, Norm. As I told him last night, I am in this whether I like it or not." She walked into the living room. "Whether you like it or not."

"This okay with you?"

Tita stared at me, wanting to say more, but waited to see where I was going.

137

"We may need her." I went inside and poured more coffee in my cup.

"Why's that?" Norm followed me and finished the coffee.

"She's an attorney."

"Damn, I would never have guessed, Counselor."

"Why, because I'm a Puerto Rican woman?" She had been misjudged before, but her words didn't confront him.

"Naw, I've known female attorneys before, but never knew Mick to associate with them."

She smiled. "Do you know his full name?"

"Mick's?"

"Yes."

"Liam Michael Murphy."

"Do you know why they call him Mick instead of Liam?"

"You've got me there, Counselor."

"Mick used to take my brother, Paco, to South Boston on Saint Patrick's Day," she began her story. "This is back when the shanty Irish were threatened by Puerto Ricans because we were all after the same manual-labor jobs. Behind his back Paco heard the Irish guys call him Spick, but he stuck it out with his friend, here. I heard him talking to Mick one night at home about it. Actually, they were laughing about it. Mick told him how the Boston Puritans used to call the Irish Micks."

"But you can't insult the Irish, at least the damn Puritanical Brits can't," I cut in and their stares told me to shut up.

"That's what he told Paco, too. So I started calling him Mick and Paco called him Mick at Harvard and it stuck," she smiled, maybe remembering a better time in her life. "Then I listened to all the stories Paco told of him, crazy things he did in college. Protesting this, demonstrating for that, always something. We called him crazy."

"Trying to save the world back then, too, was he?"

"I don't know about the world, but he was trying to save

Boston," she said. "He lost Boston, so maybe he decided to take on the world."

"You've got that right," Norm said.

"One night he and Paco and some friends were planning something. I don't remember what it was, but I thought it was too dangerous for my brother and said to Mick, 'you're mad, Mick Murphy.' And that soon got around the campus and he became Mad Mick Murphy." She laughed remembering.

"That's more than I've ever known about him. Thank you," Norm said. "Mad Mick Murphy. Now that makes sense." Norm checked his watch. "You know, ten, fifteen years ago, Mick was an award-winning journalist for all his stories from Central America. He wouldn't take a staff job on any of the news weeklies."

"My brother has kept up with Mick."

"We in a hurry?" I said.

"We need to meet some people at the Sands Beach Club. Do you know where it is?"

"The end of Simonton. Who are we meeting there?"

My cell phone rang. It was Richard.

"Hello."

"Mick, where are you?"

"Good morning to you, too, Richard. What can I do for you?"

"I just got a call from the morgue. I think this may be getting out of hand." His voice was edgy. "I'm beginning to agree with you about these guys."

He was going to tell me something I already knew, but hadn't shared with anyone.

"What did they tell you, Richard?"

Norm and Tita got up and walked to me.

"They haven't identified the bodies." He stopped there.

"But," I said.

"They were two women," his voice almost broke. "It has to

139

be them, doesn't it?"

"Have you been over to talk with Michelle?"

"She was still sedated this morning, but I'm on my way there now, with Luis. You don't sound surprised."

I didn't know what to say.

"I had a bad feeling when Julio found them. But I hoped for something else."

"You didn't hope hard enough," he said. "This is turning into a shit storm."

"What are you going to do about it?"

"I'm going to have Michelle ID the men in the photos, now that she's had some rest. If she does, I'm putting out a BOLO and fuck Smith and Jones, let them try something," he hung up.

A BOLO is police lingo for be on the look out and with the photos of two of the *gusanos* the local cops had a pretty good chance of arresting them, if they were in Key West. Once issued, the BOLO would also go out to the sheriff deputies throughout the county.

"What is it?" Tita asked, able to read my expression.

"The two bodies on the boat were female," I looked at her and it took a moment to register.

I hadn't seen the look of pure horror on a face in ten years, but there was no mistaking Tita's expression. She began to cry silently, ran to my room, and closed the door before we could hear her sobs.

Twenty-Two

"Too coincidental." Norm called room service for another pot of coffee. "When I heard about the fire last night, I knew it had to be them. But why that boat?"

I told him about the Cuban in the parking lot. He checked his watch and signed for the coffee when it came. We poured a cup each and went on the patio. The sun was shining, and it was already a warm January morning. The sky was a bright blue with only a few thin clouds sailing across it. The air held the scent of jasmine and saltwater.

"I wondered about the bodies."

"We did, too. Tita thought it might have been the Cubans."

"That would've been nice, but guys like these don't make too many mistakes."

"They killed Tom and that's gonna turn into a big mistake."

Norm checked his watch again.

"Are we in a hurry?" I got another cup coffee.

"Yes and no," he said. "Does the airport have long-term parking?"

"Yeah."

"We need to put your Jeep there and get a taxi to shuttle us around. Do you know anyone you can trust to keep their mouth shut?"

"Why a taxi and not your rental?"

"This is a tourist town and they're looking for you, your Jeep." He poured us more coffee. "As soon as the news comes out and you're not mentioned, they'll be looking for you. Taxis are for tourists and it should take a while before they check on them," he was thinking aloud, more than talking to me, "and if they check the airport and find the Jeep, they might assume you left."

It was ten-fifteen. I turned on the TV to CNN and we watched the news and drank coffee while we waited for Tita. During a commercial, I called the cab company and asked if Mike Sweet was working. He was and I told dispatch to have him call me. A half hour later, my cell chirped.

"Mike Sweet," came from the phone.

"Mick Murphy," I answered back. "You want an all-day fare?"

"To do what?"

"Shuttle me and some friends around and not talk about it."

"Fifty bucks an hour and I'll do almost anything you want."

"Are you in the van?"

"How many friends do you have?"

"I like the van."

"I'm driving the van. Where are you?"

"Meet me at the airport's long-term parking lot, at eleven-forty-five, be on time."

"I'm always on time," he laughed. "See you there," he ended the call.

"He gets fifty an hour," I said. "Now what?"

"We give Tita a few more minutes and then we leave her and go to the Sands."

"We'll give her 'till eleven-fifteen." I didn't want her to be alone and I didn't want her tagging along; I had no idea which I wanted less.

"Okay." He called room service and ordered a mixed fruit plate. "I'm hungry."

"You have a lunch date at the Sands?"

"Bob and Burt are bringing some friends, your friends, too, I guess, to help us."

The fruit plate arrived and he offered to share it. I took a few pieces of apple.

"I don't want them involved, I told you that." Three crazed killers could unravel our world very quickly and I didn't need any more of that.

"Mick, we're in the middle of nowhere," he ate and talked between bites. "I'm three thousand miles away from any contacts I can call on, so what we have left are your friends."

"They have no idea what we're dealing with and I don't want anything happening to them." I had dreams of finding another friend beaten and bloodied. "They've been known to do foolish things."

"I've dealt with foolish before," he looked at me. "I need them for surveillance. Only surveillance," he stressed. "With a little luck, Smith and Jones and crew don't know where we are. Of course, we don't know where they are, either. But, we need to find them first. You have to stay out of sight, they probably know about Michelle, so that leaves the others on the street to locate 'em."

"Can't Smith and Jones trace your credit card charges?"

"Trust me, they can't trace this card."

"Okay, but I don't like hiding."

"Look at it this way," he said. "If they're out looking for you, they can't be hiding from us, so think of it as a clever ploy to bring the bad guys out."

I finished my coffee, the pot was empty, the fruit was gone, and I laughed. "Sounds like an idea to me, but I don't know if it's a clever ploy."

He was about to say something when Tita came out of the room, her eyes were red from crying. We sat in our chairs and didn't say anything.

"These *gusanos*," she spoke more to Norm than to me, "you

think you can catch them?"

"I don't know, maybe." Norm stared at me. "Why?"

"I want this to come to an end . . . I can't go on worrying about them and the two girls deserve justice." She was anxious and beginning to sound like Padre Thomas. "Michelle deserves justice, closure."

"Counselor, let me explain something to you about these people and their handlers." He stood up and walked to a small refrigerator I hadn't noticed and took two cigars out of a box on top of it. He cut the tips of them and handed me one. He lit his and then held his lighter out to me. "These guys will never make it into your court system. It doesn't work that way."

I lit my cigar and listened. Tita sat in Norm's chair. He paced the room.

"If we help the police catch them, they will," her voice trailed off and I think she realized she was wrong. "They can't get away with this, they can't."

"People get away with a lot worse," Norm put the cigar in his mouth as he talked. "They always have and they always will."

"Murder? You are telling me they can get away with murder?" She was trying to convince herself that her rules ruled.

"Yes." He walked to the patio door and looked outside. "It's beautiful here, I can see why Mick stayed," he turned to look at her. "If either of you were as smart as you think you are, you'd leave town, maybe never come back. Or at least wait until whatever's gonna happen in Cuba goes down."

"And let them walk away?" she challenged.

"They'll get theirs, in the end. But that won't satisfy you, will it?"

"No," she said. "Why are they trying to kill Mick? Why did they kill Tom?"

"My guess?"

She nodded.

"They were looking for something to do while they waited here and heard about the sailboat race to Havana." He puffed on the cigar. "Probably drank all night and decided to make an example of someone at the sail club. Your friend Tom, he was in the wrong place at the wrong time. They were doing something *'para la causa!'*" He stood at attention for a moment of emphasis.

"What about me?" I asked.

"You were unlucky enough to know Bob, who knows Lu, who happened to overhear some obnoxious men bragging and your curiosity had you follow up when you got the photos." He went back to looking out the open patio door. "It shouldn't have gone any further, but you know the Police Chief, who ran the names and brought you to the attention of the Feds. So now, you have become a problem that has to be removed."

"What about Michelle and her friends, how'd they get involved?" Tita was unable to take her eyes off Norm.

"Probably sport for them, while they wait for whatever it is that's going to happen." He walked back into the room. "When Michelle escaped, they needed to do something, so somehow they figured if the girls died on Mick's boat, he'd be in enough trouble to be kept out of their way."

"You make it sound so easy," Tita said.

"That's the problem with evil, Counselor, it is easy and it's all around us," he looked at his watch. "Don't we have to be at the airport in half an hour?"

It was almost eleven-fifteen.

"Tita, you stay here," I said. "I'll come back, I promise."

"You promised me that when I was a teenager and you lied," she got up. "If I can be of help, I will."

Norm got a cold, distant look on his face, the look he went to when he had to tell a truth to someone that may not want to hear it. "Counselor, you know what we're going to do, when we catch them? They won't make it to jail."

"Well then, it looks like you both may need legal advice along the way," she headed to the door. "Are you coming?"

Her behavior indicated how scared she was and how badly she wanted to take back control of her life. Her attitude frightened me because Mel had the same manner in Tijuana and one nightmare in my life was more than enough.

Mike Sweet met us at the airport on time and drove us to the Sands Beach Club in the taxi-van with tinted windows. He made us put out our cigars before we got in. The Sands is a large, friendly bar and restaurant with a larger sand beach. Tables with umbrellas take up part of the outdoors and then there are lounge chairs on the sand for swimmers and sunbathers. The restaurant looks south, and if you have a good imagination, you can stare and see the lights of Havana in the evening; it takes a lot of imagination.

Large, open doors let diners inside look out at the beach and water. Ceiling fans swirl air-conditioned air before it escapes to the beach. Tables for two and four fill the indoor tiled floor and a large lobster tank sits by the entrance, and guests get to choose which Maine lobster they want. The large circular bar is often busy with locals and tourists. A row of TVs sits on a shelf that runs along the back wall and sports fans hoot and holler from the bar whenever a game is on.

Bob had two round tables put together outside in a corner on the beach for us and sat with Burt and Padre Thomas, when we walked in at noon. Ten menus, tall glasses, and a pitcher of iced tea waited for guests on the table. They were surprised to see Tita. Bob poured the tea for us and I introduced Mike Sweet to them.

"You write that column for the *Herald*?" Burt handed Mike his tea.

"Key West Taxi, you read it?" He sat down.

"Yeah, it's pretty good."

Norm and I lit what remained of our cigars and no one said anything about Tita being there.

"Who else is coming?" I asked.

"Lu, Murdock, Barraza and Doug," Bob glanced at Tita.

Rick Murdock and Dan Barraza were competitors in the titty-bar business.

"You know these guys, too?" Norm stared out at the blue ocean.

"Yeah. Why them?"

"Lu knows most of the bartenders in town, Doug's at the dock where their go-fast is, and all the perverts show up at the titty bars," Bob said.

"And I know a lot of people on Duval," Padre Thomas smiled.

"They're going to be our surveillance team," Norm scanned the table. "Lu has seen them at her bar twice in the last couple of weeks, so we know they stop at one bar on Duval Street."

"Probably coming out of the Red Garter." Lu walked to the table and sat next to Bob. "They see themselves as ladies' men." Her long black hair hung down her back. She wore shorts and a tank top and had every head in the place turning as she walked in.

Lu handed Bob an envelope that had a couple of dozen head shots of the two Cubans and he passed them around. Padre Thomas took one of each. Rick Murdock and Dan Barraza came in together and sat down. Doug arrived at twelve-fifteen, he had to pull a chair from another table. They were only expecting ten and Tita made it eleven.

After everyone ordered lunch, Norm took over the conversation. Our location, off to the side, offered us a small privacy, as long as we weren't too loud.

"These are two of the three guys we're looking for." He passed out the head shots to Rick and Dan. "These are bad

147

guys, don't kid yourself because they're smiling. They come into your place all you have to do is call my cell." He gave his cell number out and everyone recorded it into their cell phone's memory. "Don't talk to them, don't make any contact with them."

"What if they leave?" Rick asked.

"When you call me, I'll drop whatever I am doing and be on my way." Norm leaned toward Rick. "I won't be more than a few minutes, so if they've gone, I'll be close behind. Don't do anything foolish, these guys are killers."

"These are the guys who killed Tom?" Dan asked.

"And two women," Tita said.

"Yes they are," Norm said as lunch arrived.

Small talk filled the table conversation as we ate. Tita and I devoured our cheeseburgers and fries.

"You guys have the titty bars, right?" Norm was trying to put locations with names and faces.

"Mine's on Duval," Rick bit into his fish sandwich.

"Mine's on Truman," Dan wiped his mouth with a napkin. "Our bartenders are sharp, they need to be to be in our business, and our bouncers are big."

"These guys," Rick held up one of the photos, "if they think of themselves as ladies' men, they'll show up at one of our places, or the Red Garter."

Lu nodded in agreement. "I think they stop at Rick's after they leave the Garter, it's usually late when they come in."

"Lu, you have other bartenders around the island keeping an eye out for them?"

"Yes," she smiled. "I'll pass the photos around to some friends and they'll call me and I'll call you. If these guys are on Duval, one of us is going to see them."

"That's what we're hoping for."

TWENTY-THREE

Bob went with Lu to her car as Rick and David left, with photos and promises to have their employees keep an eye out for the *gusanos*.

Some still call Rick's and Dan's businesses strip clubs, but there is very little to strip off when the girls step onto the small, mirrored stage to gyrate on a shinny silver pole, clothed mostly in colored lights. The nights of old-fashioned striptease, Gypsy Rose Lee and burlesque, can be seen on the late-late show, but not in today's titty bars. The girls dance naked, provocatively, for male patrons to stick dollar bills under their garters, between their pressed-together surgically enlarged breasts and other crevices.

The clubs have been in slow decline in Key West for some time. A large titty bar had existed for less than a year where we gathered for our lunch meeting. The new proprietor spent a small fortune remodeling, eliminating the interior darkness he inherited. It had been stocked with Eastern European women, many of them Russian or Czech who spoke very little English. It closed, as did one of Dan's competitors on Truman Avenue, and another small, hidey-hole club in an alley off Front Street in Old Town.

The girls pay the club owner about one hundred dollars a night to dance for tips. The competition between the dancers, to make the evening profitable, grows in raunchiness as the liquor-driven hormones of the patrons explode. More money changes hands as the exposed lady leads an aroused patron to a small room backstage for a lap dance, where she wiggles naked on his lap for five minutes and he is often allowed to touch her, something forbidden while she's dancing on stage.

Today, rumors thrive that the Russian Mafia controls the Eastern European girls and circulates groups of them between American cities. If the dancers had any innocence when they began the circuit, it was gone when they arrived in Key West, but their youthful enthusiasm still jingled on the stage, if only briefly.

All this resulted in a tough business that needed roughness to deal with overexcited patrons every night of the week. The pretty blonde, wearing only a smile, could turn bitchy when an unwelcome, low-tipping customer groped her; customers were supposed to pay extra for groping, during the expensive lap dance. A brute of a bouncer would come to her rescue if the groping took place on stage.

I never thought of the bouncer as Sir Lancelot, riding his white horse to the rescue; no, the club couldn't allow one patron to get away with groping because soon it would be out of control and no one would be buying drinks. The club made its money off the dancers' fee, a cover charge on weekends and holidays and overpriced liquor every night. It was all about money, not the dancers or customers. Controlling the zoo was mandatory, even in Key West. This meant that Rick and Dan hired muscle-bound bouncers that kept crowds from becoming rowdy, and they were observant, always looking for the first signs of trouble.

If the *gusanos* walked into any of the city's titty bars, the bouncers would recognize two of them from the photos, and Norm would get a call. It was a good plan, I had to admit, and kept confrontation away from my friends.

"I have contacts at the small marinas on Stock Island." Burt finished his ice tea. "I'm going over and look around. Where will you be in a couple of hours?"

"Call my cell." Norm stubbed out his cigar.

"That's not a bad idea," Doug cut into the conversation. "Their go-fast hasn't left Conch Harbor, so if they have another boat it has to be slipped somewhere."

"We know it was anchored off Christmas Tree Island." I poured tea in my glass.

"They probably moved it." Doug held his glass out and I filled it. "You think it's thirty feet?"

"From what Michelle said about cabins, that's my guess, maybe bigger." Norm took a cold French fry off his plate. "Why?"

"They'd need a dinghy, to get back and forth from wherever they moved."

"The dinghy docks!" Why hadn't I thought of that? "But you would have seen them, if they used your docks."

"The city has dingy docks at both Key West and Garrison Bights." Doug pushed his chair back and stood up. "You need to buy a permit to use them, but they could've put in at Schooner Wharf and been left alone, for a while."

"Maybe they're living on a boat," Norm looked at me. "I suppose you have a few marinas around here."

"Yeah, but not where you can live aboard for more than seven days a month," I said. "You've got where I live, Garrison Bight, and then Peninsular, Safe Harbor and Oceanside marinas on Stock Island for live-aboard boaters."

"Yeah, but marinas turn a blind eye to live aboards." Doug slapped me on the back, a reminder that he knew I first lived illegally at Garrison Bight. "Right?"

"That's what I hear. Will you check out the dingy docks along the waterfront?"

"Sure. I've met all three Cubans, so I have that advantage and I've been known to spend an hour or so at Schooner in the afternoon. If I get a hint of anything, I'll call." He walked out with Burt.

Norm paid the bill and Mike Sweet thanked him.

"How long do you want me for?" He counted the money Norm gave him. "Ten hours, okay." It was an easy five hundred dollars for Mike.

"We'll want you tomorrow, too," Norm handed him another hundred. "Not much work, but we need you available, maybe this afternoon."

"I am on a short leash." He drove us to Schooner Wharf and gave Norm his cell number. "I know a few hotel concierges, I'll chat with them and show the photos around." He drove away.

Norm decided that it was best no one knew we were at the Pier House. I didn't agree, but let him have his way; after all, he was the pro and I was a Key West boat bum that had forgotten much of what I'd learned from him. It was his job to be suspicious, even of my friends. He came from a world where you trusted no one, and black and white didn't exist. If I was his friend, I was his only one.

Padre Thomas went to his favorite table by the T-shirt booth. You couldn't see the stage, but had full view of the dock and piers, as well as the bar.

"Kalik, Kalik, Bud, for me," Thomas counted off. "What would you like, Tita?" He was going for the beers; this would cost one of us.

"Coke," she rarely drank in the afternoons.

He passed the drinks out and sat. "I can help, too," he sipped from his beer and lit a cigarette. "I'm familiar with many of the street actors on Duval."

The city of Key West is inundated with homeless men and women escaping the cold north every winter; many hassle visitors for money, clogging the sidewalks of Old Town; others sleep in public parks and defecate wherever they please, and the chamber of commerce demanded the city do something about the situation. The city commission passed a no panhandling code in an attempt to get the beggars off Old Town sidewalks. The survivalists among them quickly resorted to being street artists, a trade the city had allowed for years. Street corners along Duval began to display musicians with questionable talent, pirates in torn, smelly rags and bent swords, and men spray painted silver, who tried to stand motionless like human statues, but found it difficult as the alcohol shakes began.

"Thomas, I don't think we want to get the homeless involved," I said.

"Why?"

"Yeah, why?" Norm got up and bought us two cigars from the old Cuban who rolled them in his kiosk. He lit his before he handed me one. "They have eyes."

"Yeah, and mouths," I cut the cigar and lit it, using my lighter. "For a drink or a few bucks they'd sell their mothers."

"Not all of them, Mick." Thomas crushed out his cigarette. "There are some good people on the street, they're not all bums."

"I've represented some of them." Tita sipped her Coke. "A lot of people in Key West are only a payday or two away from being homeless. Some, if they lose a roommate will be homeless. It's not a disease, you won't catch it," she laughed. "You live on a boat and the State of Florida's health system considers you among the homeless, Mick."

She made her point and I shut up.

"Padre, I'll give you some money and you pass it out, in small increments, like fives, and tell them there's a reward of fifty to the person who first spots the Cubans," Norm peeled money off his bankroll.

"How are they gonna call you, Norm? Most homeless don't carry cell phones." I puffed on the cigar and sipped my beer.

"I'll make myself more visible tonight," Padre Thomas lit another cigarette.

We drank our beers while we watched the tourists walk along and stare at the tall ships. It was the beginning of the weekend, and season had begun, so the island would be packed. Michael McCleod's voice blanketed the bar, as he told stories about old Key West and sang his songs.

"Padre, is that all you can do?" Norm sipped from his beer. "I hear you talk to angels."

Padre Thomas stared at me for a second and then smiled at Norm.

"What else have you heard?"

"Some think it's a scam you use to get free drinks," Norm winked at me. "What's Mick think?"

"Sometimes he believes me."

"He's been known to be superstitious," Norm blew thick smoke rings. "I think he still believes in Leprechauns."

"Are you superstitious?" Padre Thomas inhaled deeply and then stubbed out the cigarette.

"Not really," Norm said. "But I will tell you why I might believe in angels."

"Please, tell us."

"Okay, then, I believe the devil exists, we see his evil every day. If he exists, then God has to, too, since you can't have one without the other."

"And your point is?" Tita chewed ice from her Coke.

"My point is I have determined that there is a devil, I've seen his work all around the world. The devil exists, so I have to believe God exists. I don't believe organized religion has it right. And Lucifer was an angel, a fallen angel, so you could say I believe in angels, because I believe there's a devil."

"I still don't know what your point is." Tita finished her Coke and chewed on another piece of ice. "You make it almost sound as if you prefer Lucifer."

I had purposely put off telling Norm about Padre Thomas and his angels, but Bob and Burt must have said something to him last night, because he seemed to know all about them.

"I know what to expect from Lucifer, I know where he stands. But when I'm talking with someone who communicates with angels, and I'm in a shit-pot of trouble, I am curious to see what they have to say about the situation." Norm got up and went to the bar. He came back with a Coke for Tita and three beers. "I've dealt with Inca and Mayan shamans with surprising results, so why not a priest who sees angels?"

Padre Thomas lit another cigarette. No one said anything; we listened to the music and loud bar conversations around us and drank our beers.

"It's curious that Bob thinks I use the angels to get free drinks," Thomas finally said. "It's always someone else that brings up angels as a topic, and then I'm accused of talking about them. Like this beer," he held the bottle up. "We're talking about angels and you bought me a beer. I didn't start this conversation or ask for the beer. It doesn't matter if they believe or not, they want to know."

I had not been aware that he knew about Bob's opinion of him, and I don't know why it surprised me that he did know.

"I am open to believing, if you can tell me something that isn't hocus-pocus, Padre." Norm took a long swallow of beer and puffed on his cigar. "I learned a long time ago to never discourage help of any kind."

"I've told Mick the three men he is looking for are the men who killed Tom."

Norm looked at me with a cold expression. "This is the information you had and asked me to take you on faith?"

"Yeah, I didn't think you'd believe me."

"You're probably right. What else?" he turned to Thomas.

"I told Mick they'd kill again."

Norm and Tita stared at me.

"Padre, this is all behind us. What do you have about the future?" Norm waited for an answer.

"You think angels can tell the future?" Padre Thomas lit another cigarette.

"I don't know what they can do."

"Neither do I, but I know they're real and they've helped me."

"Will they help us?"

"They'll help me, help you, I think."

"Hocus-pocus, Padre. Tell us something before the Cubans kill again, before they kill one of us."

TWENTY-FOUR

I didn't understand Norm's declaring his belief in angels. In the past, I had seen him encourage actions by people I knew he opposed, but it always helped him accomplish his task. What could he be trying to get from Padre Thomas? Possibly, he thought Thomas was an enemy, but I didn't see why or how he could come to that conclusion. Did he see something I didn't? The idea that he believed in angels never entered my mind, because I've known him long enough, and seen him in too many volatile situations to accept his conversation on angels at face value.

Padre Thomas took Norm's money and promised to spread it around to the street people.

"I'll be up and down Duval until I have news," he promised. "If you're not at the Pier House, I'll call Mick's cell," and he left.

"Did you tell him we were staying at the Pier House?" Norm's suspicious eyes followed Padre Thomas as he walked down the pier, looking more like a lost soul than a conspirator.

"No." I looked at Tita.

"I didn't say anything."

"Sometimes he knows things and I can't figure out how," I said.

"That's when you believe in the angels?"

"It's an explanation."

"You guys are driving me crazy. Who are you expecting?" Tita raised her voice as she chewed a piece of ice and her words made no sense.

I looked at Norm and then we both stared back at Tita. I didn't know what I was doing that bothered her.

"What are you talking about?" I finished my beer and relit my cigar.

"After we sat down, first Norm and then you," her voice grew anxious, "your eyes kept moving, searching for something, I was getting a headache watching both of you. It was like you wanted to make sure no one saw us together."

"I don't know what you're talking about," I said.

"A necessary precaution in a situation like this." Norm relit his cigar. "You are always examining your surroundings, looking for signs of trouble without being too obvious. Did you catch the fat, bald guy at the bar, with the stringy mouse tail, who's been looking over here off and on?"

Tita turned to the bar.

"Yeah," I didn't turn, I kept talking to Norm. Without realizing it, I had been searching the bar for the *gusanos*. Some old habits don't die. "Snooper Scooper."

"That his name or job title?"

"That's what Mick calls him." Tita turned back to the table. "He's a newspaper publisher."

"Bullshit, a newspaper publisher, he writes crap, going after people that can't do anything about it. A speck of truth and he fills the rest with innuendo and rumor. He's no journalist, either."

"First Amendment, I thought you were a big supporter of it."

"For journalists, not people who take advantage of it, exploit it for their own popularity."

Scooper got his courage up, probably after a few beers, and headed toward our table.

"Brother Mick," he mumbled the words.

Darrel Coppersmith, alias Snooper Scooper, named after the

dog and cat poop scoop sold in pet stores, is as round as he is short. His large ears make his bald, chubby head look like a hairless Mickey Mouse ornament. A poor excuse for a ponytail threads down the back of his fat neck. The masthead on his weekly rag is yellow, and fittingly so. He attacks governments and public officials, knowing they have no recourse to his exaggerations. He once told me that he always wrote the truth and could prove it. I challenged him, and he said if he didn't write the truth why hadn't someone sued him? I laughed at him, because he hasn't a pot to piss in, so there's nothing to get by suing him, that's why. What little money he gets from advertising he spends on drink and lives off a woman, who we all thought should know better. In Scooper's case, love wasn't only blind it was dumb.

"Scooper, how many times do I have to tell you we're not brothers?" I turned away from him.

"I haven't met your friend." He reached to shake hands.

"And you ain't gonna, go away." I knocked his hand from the table.

"Did you see today's issue?" He ignored the insult and put a liquor smile on his silly red face.

"You know I don't read that rag." I exhaled heavy cigar smoke at him.

"Rumor is you've got Cubans tied in to Tom's murder and the cops aren't cooperating," he spoke slowly, thinking each word through before he spit it out. Many drunks do that, thinking it makes them sound smart. "I could help you there, get them off their asses."

"You want to help me, go away."

He put his hand on one of the empty chairs, as if he was going to sit down. Norm stretched his leg out and hooked the chair. Scooper tried to pull it away from the table, looked at me and then realized Norm held it.

"I have my sources, even in the police department, so I know what's going on," he threatened in a drunk's voice.

With a heavy Spanish accent Norm said, "Where I come from we use nuisances like you for chum." His voice was cold and his potent stare scared Scooper, who backed off and returned to his seat at the bar.

Tita and I laughed at the scene.

"Chum?" I laughed.

"I don't know, I looked at him and he reminded me of a big bucket of bloody chum on a fishing boat." Norm crushed his cigar in the ashtray.

My cell phone chirped; it was Richard Dowley.

"Hello, Richard."

"Mick, Michelle identified the two men," his voice was uneasy. I thought he was having second thoughts about the BOLO and the response it would get from Smith and Jones. "I'm on the way to the station to issue the BOLO. I am also meeting with the state attorney to go after arrest warrants." He could have issued the BOLO from his car.

"How is she doing?"

"She doesn't know about her friends. I don't want to tell her until we can get positive IDs," he sounded tired. "One of the crisis counselors was able to get some personal information from her, so I need to call her folks," he stopped talking and I thought we had been cut off. "This is the worst part of my job," he finally said. "I don't know how anyone ever gets used to it."

"You need dental records to ID the bodies?" I didn't know what else to say.

"I need to tell one set of parents their daughter is safe and then tell two others that we think their kids are dead, I need their dental records. You know how cold that sounds, no matter how you say it."

"Do it, get it over with, that's my only advice," I said.

"No autopsy results yet," he hesitated. "When the BOLO goes out, you could be in trouble. These guys are major fuck-ups."

"Richard, I think I'm already in trouble."

"I think you're right. I'll be in touch." He hung up.

"He's going to issue a BOLO for the Cubans," I told them about the brief conversation.

No one wanted any more to drink. The wind had picked up and the bar smelled like salt and seaweed, more than spilled beer and cigarette smoke. Clouds filled the afternoon sky and the westward clouds were dark and filled with rain.

"What's with this weather? Is it going to rain every night?"

"Hey, it's following you from California," I joked. "Don't complain."

"A Friday night rain," Norm said as we stood, "that should clear people off the street."

"Not Duval Street," I said as we walked by the Sebago Catamarans. "It's just water, and if you drink inside, it doesn't get in your beer."

"I told Bob I would meet him at Rick's at eight, Lu's bartending." We walked around the Conch Farm Restaurant and onto Front Street. "Maybe on a night like this the Cubans will show up to get out of the rain."

"And if they do?" We were outside Pat Croce's Pirate Soul Museum, across from the Pier House, when Tita asked.

Norm ignored her, advice I would have given him, if he had asked.

"You stay in the hotel," he said to me. "By now they have to know you weren't connected to the boat fire and the girls' deaths. I don't know how good Smith and Jones are, but they have people looking for you."

"Why? How do you know this?" Tita wouldn't be ignored again.

"They'll hold Mick responsible for the BOLO, for one thing. He knows what they're up to and they can't have too much of that going around."

"The Police Chief knows, too," I said.

"There is that." Norm checked his watch. He had plenty of time before he had to meet Bob. "Smith and Jones probably still think he's controllable. But, my guess is, the Cubans would kill all of you. Smith and Jones are trying to control them, and, who knows, it may already be out of their hands."

"That wouldn't be good," I said.

"No, that would be bloody."

"How can you talk so calmly about this? This is Key West, we're in America, you talk as if it's the Wild West. There are laws . . ."

"Counselor," the word came out sternly, "you go back and stay at the hotel. It's best, believe me."

"And what, ignore what you're doing?"

"Think of Michelle and her two friends," he said coldly. "Think about when you noticed the fire at the marina. Where were you? I'll tell you where, you were on the boat the Cubans wanted to torch, and if they had gotten the right boat, we wouldn't be having this conversation."

Tita's complexion paled. I had seen people look like she did just before seasickness kicked in. She ran across the street and into the hotel's parking lot.

"This is up to you and me," he said as we both watched her run away. "Your friends can't do it."

"Yeah, I know. But first we need to find the Cubans."

"I have to find them, you need to keep off the street so they continue to look for you. When I've located them, I'll call and we'll come up with a plan to kill 'em."

"What if they're all together? What if Smith and Jones are there, too?"

"We may only get one opportunity, we'll have to take it."

Norm left me outside the Pirate Soul and walked to Duval and turned into the crowd, beginning his search, waiting for the phone call that would put an end to all this.

Twenty-Five

Tita waited for me in the crowded parking lot of the Pier House, crying. She pushed me away when I tried to place my arm around her and we walked to the room without speaking. Dark clouds rolled across the sky, promising more rain. Once inside the suite, Tita went into the bathroom. When she came out, her face had its color back and she tried to smile.

"Norm has a dynamic presence." She looked out at the harbor and the beginning of the rain. "I don't think I like him."

She let me hug her when I got to the patio door.

"Can he do the things he was talking about?" she whispered the words as if we were in a crowd.

"Yes," was all I said.

"Is he right? Are there different laws for people like him?"

"Yes." We watched boats lose the race with the weather as they headed to port.

"I must have been out the day it was discussed in class." She looked up at me and forced a smile. "He's paid with tax dollars?"

"Probably." We watched the rain as the wind blew it sideways.

Tita opened the patio door and a cool salt breeze swept in.

"Smith and Jones, the two agents you met, the government pays them, too?"

"Yes." I hugged her closer and could still smell her shampoo. "Tita, there is a James Bond world, minus the gadgets and martinis, out there. In our government, in the Mexican govern-

164

ment, I have to assume in all governments. Didn't you read anything about the secret wars in Southeast Asia during Vietnam? Or anything about the Israeli Mossad?"

"Yes." She pulled away and walked onto the patio and into the rain. "But we were at war, the Israelis are at war. It's different."

"It's about men and power." I pulled her out of the rain and we went back inside. "Someday, maybe all the abuses our government was involved in in Central America will come out. Think about what it took for Regan to send American government officials to Iran with Irish passports. Today, that Marine asshole that violated our Constitution is a hero." I closed the patio door because the wind was getting chilly. "Watergate . . ."

"I was thinking of that." She picked up the room service menu. "I wasn't even a teenager, but I remember how angry Paco would get when he read the newspapers or watched the news. So, it really isn't new, not really, is it? Certain people can tread on our rights and we are helpless to do anything about it, Constitution be damned."

"Yes. Whatever agency Smith and Jones are with will have deniability if the operation screws up. Maybe they will be telling the truth, maybe they won't. Somewhere in the bowels of Washington, Norm's agency knows what he's doing, but they will put some distance between him and them. And, it may not be for the public, it may be for the agency Smith and Jones are with, for when this is all over. It may not make the news, it might just go away."

"What will happen to Norm?" She called room service and ordered filet mignon, rare, with the works for both of us. "When all this is over, I mean."

"He's a pro, with too many good jobs completed for them to do anything to him."

"By jobs, you mean killings?"

165

"I've witnessed him risk his life to save innocent people, when he could have acted differently, but yes, he has killed people and I don't know how he deals with it. He doesn't discuss it with me. Hell, maybe he really believes in angels. Thomas told me the other day that angels are God's warriors."

"I don't see Norm as an angel, but I hope he's going back to California when this is over, angel warrior or not." The idea concerned her, I could tell by her expression. "Are you going with him?"

"His life is back in California, so he's gonna go home," I said. "My life is here, so I'm not going anywhere."

"Will it be the same?" She wanted to know how all this would affect her.

"I can't answer that. Life influences all of us in different ways. We haven't been affected as dramatically as Michelle has, but having met her the way we did, has changed us all. My finding Tom has shocked my system, changed my world."

"Norm expects you to help him, have you helped him in the past?"

I still didn't feel it was the time for me to talk about Mel and how she died in Tijuana, but I did tell her about the few times Norm had come to my rescue because I'd gotten too deeply into a dicey story about drug lords or guerilla wars.

"I've never been part of any of his operations, if that's what you're thinking." Room service knocked and set up our meal on the table.

"Why are you carrying a gun?" She put salt on her steak and potatoes.

"Because someone is trying to kill me."

"Can you use it? More important, will you use it?" She picked at her salad.

"If I have to."

We ate in silence. I got sodas from the suite's refrigerator.

One Duval, the restaurant at the Pier House, serves excellent food and is a throwback to old Key West, with a view of the harbor that makes its menu prices worth it. Our steaks were wonderful.

"What do we do now?" She put the dishes on the room service cart. "Wait for him to call, so you can run out?"

"If he can find them, I guess."

"If he's as good as you say, he probably will. It's a small island."

"They could be gone, or maybe Smith and Jones got some sense when Richard filed the BOLO."

"You're not making me feel any better by lying to me." She looked out at the rain. "I need a change of clothes, can you walk me home?"

"We're supposed to stay here."

"Yeah, well I've been thinking about it and I don't think they know about me. I hadn't seen you for two weeks before Tom was killed. Then, not until late Wednesday night at the Tree Bar, so how are they going to know about me or where I live?" She made a good case. "I don't want to be alone, Mick, and I can't sleep another night in these clothes. We'll walk to my place. Hell, it's raining out, so who could recognize us?"

"We'll have to use the side streets."

Tita owned a small Conch house on Frances Street, across from the cemetery. She bought the house soon after she opened her practice and said the neighbors across the street were always quiet. Today, Tita's small one hundred and seventy-five-thousand-dollar home was worth about seven hundred thousand; not a bad investment strategy for a lawyer.

We walked hand-in-hand out of the hotel onto Front Street and backtracked the route we had taken earlier from Schooner Wharf. Caroline and William Streets, in front of B.O.'s restaurant, were already flooded. We kept walking down William, across Eaton with cars driving too fast in the rain, and turned left on Southard, walking against traffic on the one-way street. The rain came down steady and we had given up the idea of staying dry.

These were the narrow streets of Old Town, lined with two-bedroom, one-bath Conch cottages like Tita's, from the early 1900s when Cuban cigar rollers lived in them. Some modern, two-story Conch-styled homes were wedged onto the tiny lots. The yards were small, but the property was valuable. Every so often there were larger two-story homes, Key West mansions, nestled into the old neighborhoods. Light shown through only half the homes' shaded windows, a result of many of them being second homes. Open porch windows let in the cool breeze and dinnertime aromas found their way to the wet sidewalks, as we passed homes where people lived.

At Frances, we turned right and walked with the cemetery across the street. Small, wet halos formed on the few scattered light poles, making the cemetery darker than usual, and the windswept rain highlighted its eeriness. Old trees sprouted in the cemetery, their large shadowy branches shaking in the wind like dozens of bony arms, added to the horror-movie effect.

"It looks creepy." I squeezed her hand and pointed across the street.

"Are you afraid of ghosts, too?"

"Should I be?"

"No, I talk with them all the time." She squeezed my hand back. "Thomas has his angels, I have my ghosts."

"What's that leave me?" We were soaked.

"You've got me or Norm, your choice."

I caught the dome light of a car parked by Tita's house go on and off. I pulled her arm and we slowed down. I glanced behind us, but saw no one. I pulled her to me and kissed her, she kissed me back.

"How romantic, in the rain and across from the cemetery, what will the ghosts think," she said.

"I saw someone get out of a car in front of your house and I don't know where they went," I tried to put urgency in my words.

"Mick, parking is a premium on these streets, they could live two blocks away. You'd know that if you came by more often." She ignored my anxiety and pulled me along.

An iron fence encircled the cemetery to keep unwanted guests out after closing, or maybe to keep the ghosts in, I'm not sure. Because the island is at sea level, crypts have been used for interment since a hurricane washed up buried caskets and floated them through Old Town more than a century ago. Much smaller than the more famous cemetery in New Orleans, the Key West cemetery is still a tourist attraction, full of distinctive mausoleums. City law requires the families of those interred at the cemetery to take care of the plots. As families moved away, or died off, sections of the cemetery have decomposed, especially the graves from when caskets were placed in the ground.

"Let's be slow," I said.

"You like getting wet?"

I didn't like the feeling I was getting and it wasn't because of the cemetery or Tita's ghosts. It was hard to see in the rain on the poorly lit street. Light feathered onto many of the small porches near her house, but her house was dark. It should have been, because there were no lights on when we left earlier. We were three houses away when I saw a shadow move on her porch. I pulled her to a stop.

"There's someone on your porch," I whispered.

"You think . . ." she began to get nervous. "What do we do?"

I knew we had stalled too long if they had identified us. I was ready to say we go back, but the windshield of the car next to us made a popping noise. I looked at it and saw the small bullet hole. I looked back toward the dark porch, saw another muzzle flash, and pulled Tita to the wet sidewalk, as a second gunshot popped the side window.

I looked behind us to see if it was safe to run, but a man was getting out of a car, and as he raised his arm, I lifted Tita off the ground and slipped between two parked cars. My arms were trembling and it wasn't from her weight.

"Is there a way into the cemetery?" I asked.

She looked at me, not believing what was happening. "The gate across from here is chained, but kids push it and can slip through."

"Okay, stay low, but run and push through and keep going to the other side," I said. "I'll be right behind you."

"No," she said firmly, "you'll be with me." She took my hand and dashed from the protection of the two cars.

I pulled my Glock, but couldn't see anything to shoot at. Where had they gone? Tita fit through the gate easily, it was a little harder for me, but a muzzle flash from across the street gave me an extra incentive and I was through.

"Run," I said, and fired toward the man slowly crossing the street.

TWENTY-SIX

Slippery grass covered the uneven ground of the cemetery and I fell once catching up to Tita. The rain was both our friend and enemy. Rain clouds darkened the night sky and the scattered streetlights outside the cemetery added to the shadowy weirdness of the landscape. Someone pulled at the metal gate. I heard the shot that broke the lock holding it closed. We stopped at a small mausoleum, three caskets high. I turned to look at the gate. It was wide open.

"Where are we going?" Tita whispered.

"To the other side, to Windsor Lane." I pulled her forward and we both tripped into a puddle over a decomposing gravesite.

We got up, moved more slowly, bent over to make ourselves less visible, and mud covered us both, now. I kept turning to see if I could find where our pursuers were. I couldn't. A lightning flash lit up the cemetery and thunder exploded above us, giving the fleeting effect of a third-rate horror movie. Tita squeezed my hand.

The cemetery was dark again, the heavy rain windswept sideways and washed some of the mud off us. We had to dodge single crypts, aged headstones, large old trees, and monuments, trying not to lose our footing. We stopped at the next large mausoleum.

"I'm shaking," Tita said.

"Me, too," I looked around, but saw nothing. "It's cold," I lied.

Windsor Lane and Olivia Street were as poorly lit as Frances Street, but a small convenience store there stayed open late. I thought of my cell, and in the moment of safety grabbed it and called Norm. I could tell from the background noise that he was in a bar, probably Rick's.

"Speak up," he said.

"Norm, I need help, Tita and I are in trouble." I talked clearly, but in a whisper.

"Where are you?" His voice became more controlled.

"At the cemetery, go to Windsor and Olivia."

"What's the problem?" I could almost see him paying this bar tab and leaving.

"Two guys are shooting at us."

"Are you shooting back?"

"I can't see them. It's dark in here."

"Okay, Mike's outside. I am on my way," he said. "Windsor and Olivia," he repeated to make sure he had it correctly.

"Yes," I said, and the phone went dead.

"Is he coming?"

"Yes, we have to move closer to Windsor." We were running parallel to Olivia.

Olivia is a one-way street and we were going against the direction of traffic. One car drove slowly down the narrow street and we froze and hid bent over by a two-story crypt. After it passed lightning flashed again, thunder boomed and we stayed hidden by the crypt. My adrenalin was running high, but Tita's anxiety was also strong. We remained frozen. I listened to the rainfall and I could hear the faint sound of a TV coming from one of the houses across the street.

I put a finger to my lips, telling her to be quiet. I stood up and looked over the top of the crypt, scanning the creepy cemetery. I heard someone speaking Spanish, but couldn't understand the words. It was coming from in front of the crypt, maybe fifty feet away. I heard a reply come from my right. They were loud and confident and I wondered what gave them the confidence.

They were getting close, too close.

I signaled Tita to stay low, but to move. I took her hand and we crept to the next, larger mausoleum. There were some small rocks on the grass. I picked up two and tossed them toward the center of the cemetery. Two voices yelled something in Spanish, sounding surprised. We flattened ourselves against the mausoleum. I could see the lights of the store. Where was Norm?

This mausoleum had a ledge on each level and was five caskets high, and six wide, one of the highest in the cemetery. Many of the thirty crypts were empty. It was the high ground and if we could get on top, I would have a good view of our surroundings.

"Tita, you have to climb to the top of this," I whispered.

"What about you?" she said nervously.

"I'm going up behind you."

Voices from two men, cussing in Spanish, came from somewhere in front of us.

"It's above their sight, we'll be safe there." I led her up past the first shelf and boosted her from behind.

The rain had made the old, painted concrete ledge slippery, but I kept one hand on her leg as I stepped up behind her. She was having difficulty. I let go of her leg and climbed up next to her. She was holding on and her fear of falling was clear. I climbed to the top. Another flash of lightning illuminated the area and from the roof of the mausoleum, I saw the two men. They had split up and were moving on either side of us.

Tita had climbed up one more step and as she did her foot kicked open one of the temporary crypt covers. Thunder covered the noise of the wood front breaking away. She lost her footing, I grabbed her wrist, and it kept her from falling backward. I got hold of her other wrist as she tried to set her feet on the slippery outcrop. She slipped and her legs went into the crypt. The motion pulled me forward, as more of her body slid into the crypt. I was half off the roof, holding her. I let one wrist go so I could support myself, and instinct had her grab the shelf above. She steadied herself, half in, half out of the crypt as I fell off the roof. I rolled with the fall, slipped on the wet grass, and hit a tombstone.

When I glanced up Tita lay on her stomach in the crypt, fear etched on her face. I used my hand to motion her to go farther in and to hide. She frantically shook her head, no. I stood up, unclipped my Glock, and felt a jolt of pain in my back. Another flash of lightning and I saw one man was off to my right. He raised his arm, as I raised mine and we both fired at the same time, the gunshot lost in the boom of thunder. He went down. Tita screamed. It meant the second man was off to my left.

I rushed to Tita. "Stay in there." I ran toward the man I had shot.

Movies have made heroes of men so capable with handguns that most people don't realize that one person shooting a gun out of the hands of another, during a shootout, is an improbability. Handguns are not accurate, especially at the distance from where I shot. That I hit the man shooting at me was a miracle, as much as his missing me was. I knew from experience that if I aimed at his chest I was just as likely to hit his kneecap or shoulder.

I kicked the man's gun away from him. He looked up at me, but said nothing. He held his stomach and used a broken tombstone as his pillow. As the rain washed down, I could see he was older, and not one of the two *gusanos* in the photo. He wasn't dead, but it wouldn't be long. Was this a robbery attempt gone bad?

A voice calling "Roberto" came from behind me. I turned, but saw no one. I kicked the fallen man's gun one more time and rushed back to the mausoleum. Tita had slid deep into the crypt and I left her there. I stayed as much in the shadows as possible and worked my way to another mausoleum. I kept an eye on the corner store, hoping to see a taxi van. I heard Roberto called again, but there was no reply.

A taxi pulled up in front of the store and the driver beeped his horn once. The windows were fogged and the wipers sloshed back and forth, but I couldn't see if it was Mike and Norm.

Lightning flashed off in the distance and I saw two men moving in the direction of the man I shot. One was farther back, moving slowly. I moved to the left of the mausoleum, hugged it, and worked my way around so I could see the two men. Thunder boomed and I felt the mausoleum vibrate. They spread out, searching for Roberto or me, maybe both of us. Where had the second man come from? Were these the three *gusanos?* Was the old man Pepe?

I bent over and hurried to a small crypt to my left, wanting to circle behind them. I slipped in another sunken grave's puddle, forced myself up, and rushed to a large grave marker. I watched as the men walked slowly past the crypt where Tita was hiding. Why was one so far behind the other? The first man found Roberto, bent down, and then looked around. He stood and turned to face the man behind him. I saw a muzzle flash and he fell backward, not far from Roberto.

My cell chirped and the noise made me jump. The readout showed it was Norm.

"Where are you?" I whispered.

"I'm standing over two dead men. I shot one, so I assume you shot the other," he said.

175

I rushed from my hiding place and called his name. He turned, he still had his gun in his hand.

"When did you get here?"

"I jumped the fence at the Sexton's office and walked this way as Mike drove down the street. Are these the guys?" He bent down and went through their pockets. He brought out two wallets.

These were not the men in Lu's photos. Who were they?

Norm pulled ID from the wallets.

"Roberto Olivarez, you shot him, and Carlos Diaz, both in their sixties." He looked down. "I'll bet you they're Cubans from the old days. They must have been hired guns."

"Why?"

"Maybe your *gusanos* are doing their thing and wanted you eliminated. Hey, where's Tita?"

I called her name and after a moment, her head popped out of the crypt. We walked toward her and saw Mike's taxi return to the store. With a little help, Tita was able to slide out. She hit me hard on the chest when she reached the ground.

"You left me in a damp crypt with caskets on either side of me," she yelled.

"It was a good hiding place." I pushed her away. "You slipped, I didn't put you in there."

"Let's get over the fence and out of here." Norm moved us toward the Windsor Lane gate.

"What about . . ." She turned to look back.

"Someone will find them in the morning." Norm kept us moving.

Twenty-Seven

Three old Conch houses, dark as tombs, butted up against the cemetery fence on Olivia Street at Windsor Lane. The wind, rain, and thunder covered whatever noise we made in the cemetery when we climbed the fence and dropped to the wet pavement. The convenience store was lit up, but closed, and Mike Sweet's taxi waited about a half block down Olivia. I think we startled him when Norm opened the van's back door, but he smiled and after we got in, Mike pulled into the rain-swept street and drove away without asking questions.

Tita looked toward her house as the van turned left on Frances. She gave a quick stare across the street to the cemetery and then it was gone, and Mike made another left onto Southard Street.

"Finnegan's," I said, and no one disagreed with me.

"You want me to wait?" He stopped in front of Finnegan's, on Grinnell Street.

The rain fell steadily and lightning flashed too far off for us to hear the thunder. We were wet and dirty and didn't care about the rain. Norm said he'd call in the morning and sent Mike home.

We entered the Irish pub at two in the morning, the dining room closed at one, but the bar had a late-night business going. Tita and Norm followed me to my favorite table against the back wall. Megan, the waitress, gave us a second look, making sure we were who she thought we were, before coming over.

"Mick," her brogue as thick as Irish potato soup. "A wee bit of damp tonight. What will you be havin'?"

"Three Irish coffees, coffee with whiskey, Megan, no sugar or fancy cream." She smiled and her freckles moved. "Two shots of Jameson's . . ."

"Make it three shots," Tita said.

"And three pints of Harp."

"Aye, Mick," and she walked to the bar.

Irish music played from hidden speakers, but loud conversations hid most of it. The stage stood empty. I was cold, so I guessed Tita was, too.

"Damn cold rain." I rubbed my hands together.

"Too much rain," Norm said.

Tita didn't say anything. Megan brought the drinks. We picked up the mugs, just to warm our hands, and sipped the liquor-laced coffee. Norm smiled after tasting the warmth of the hot whiskey, then he picked up his shot of Jameson.

"Up the rebels," Norm toasted and downed the whiskey.

Tita and I followed his example. She wrinkled her nose in expectation of the strong liquor and swallowed, leaving half the shot in her glass. She coughed and took a long unlady-like swig from the pint of Harp.

"You okay?" I put my hand on her wet shoulder, it was shaking.

"I don't know how you can drink this stuff straight." We both knew I wasn't asking about the whiskey cough. "I'm okay," she smiled and gulped the remaining whiskey.

"What happened?" Norm sipped his coffee.

I told him about walking Tita home and how the two men ambushed us as we approached her house.

"I don't know how they knew about me," Tita spoke softly and warmed her hands on the coffee mug. Her words were almost lost in the din. "I hadn't seen Mick in a couple of weeks and this all just started." She wasn't sure why this peril inserted itself into her life and she needed to latch onto something that would help her understand.

"You underestimated them." Norm finished his coffee. "That's always a mistake." His look told me he expected I would have known better.

"Has anyone called you?" My coffee was almost gone and I wanted to change the subject.

"No, maybe it's the weather." He sounded disappointed that no one from the luncheon meeting had called.

"Or they're not here. Why send two guys from Miami?"

"Obviously to kill you."

I could tell from the expression on his face that he was thinking about something.

"What's bothering you?"

"The three Cubans are killers," he gulped from his pint, accenting his words with hand gestures, "so why use anyone else to do a job they're capable of?" He turned his fingers into a figurine of a gun and pointed it at me.

"Why?" I hoped he had an explanation.

"Maybe the *gusanos* have gone back to Cuba, so the two guys in the cemetery pulled short straws and got the job." He pulled the imaginary trigger and then blew on the tip of his finger.

"They're going by boat," I said, "they wouldn't have gone with this front coming through. Not in a go-fast."

"Well then, we could be in for some real trouble. If they're bringing in more men, reinforcements, just to get you." He frowned, not accepting what he had said. "No, because that would be turning you into something bigger than you are. They've gone, I know it."

"You think the operation's going down?"

"Most likely."

"Is that a good or bad thing?" Tita asked.

"Counselor, the safest way to deal with this is to question everything Smith and Jones said to Mick or the Chief of Police," he thought aloud. "So what have they said? Their agents are Cuban military officers who deserted on orders from a general and a Communist Party official and that could be true—or not—because it doesn't affect Mick, yet. Or it could be a story Smith and Jones concocted for them."

Tita and I listened to Norm's concerns and I wondered what the truth was behind all the smoke and mirrors. Norm and I had another beer. We decided to believe the story Smith and Jones had told, until we knew otherwise and by then it might be too late.

"The rain is supposed to stop, but the winds are here for the weekend, so it might be they're not going to try this by water." He drank from the pint.

"But the winds are westerly," I said.

"So."

"Norm, the Gulf Stream flows west to east, westerly winds flatten the stream. We don't get many westerlies in the Keys, so usually when crossing the stream you have six- to eight-foot seas, three days of these winds will flatten it out for boaters and rafters."

"Okay, so they're going by boat," he said. "And maybe they're leaving from Key West, but where are they coming back to?"

"Key West, that's what Smith and Jones told Richard and me."

"Had to tell you something."

"But why lie about coming back here?" I asked.

"You brought the Cubans to the attention of the law," he continued to sip from the pint, "and they couldn't have that. So, Smith and Jones come here and bullshit you and the Chief."

"If the Cubans are gone, does it mean it's over?" Tita asked.

"Naw, I think it's personal with them, maybe more so now."

He didn't have to say anything about the two dead Cubans at the cemetery.

Norm and I finished our beers, Tita left her pint more than half full. I paid the tab and we walked back to the Pier House. The rain had stopped, but clouds filled the sky and lightning continued to flash off in the distance, above the Gulf Stream. The streets were flooded. We walked down Caroline Street with all its old and new mansions, and turned at Simonton Street. We were left to our own thoughts and walked without talking. Tita held tightly to my hand.

"I need a hot bath," she said when we got to the suite, and went to my room.

She hadn't picked up any clean clothes, but the bath seemed more important and she closed the door.

Norm grabbed two towels from his room, fell into an over-stuffed chair, and stretched out drying himself. "We might be between a rock and a hard place, Mick." He tossed me the other towel, as he took off his shirt.

"What's that mean?" I sat across from him and tried to wipe the dampness off me.

"We don't know what we're up against," he drawled, sleepily. "Are the *gusanos* here, or gone? Who the hell are the two dead guys and why were they trying to kill you?"

"You don't think they're connected?"

"You want to go with that?" He kicked off his shoes. "You okay with that?"

"Yeah, I can't think of anything else that works." I slipped my boat shoes off. They might never dry out.

"Okay," he stretched and yawned, "the *gusanos* have gone on to whatever their project is . . . bringing out the general . . . whatever. They pull this off and they're heroes, right?"

"Yeah, according to Smith and Jones, the general and communist party official call for a Cuba without Communism and then they expect the military to oust the Communists."

"You're the Caribbean scholar, can it happen?"

I thought of my friend Jose, a dissident Cuban writer, who told an American friend of mine about his willingness to take up arms to defend the revolution if the exile community tried to takeover the government. The Cuban people didn't want to change one dictatorship for another. Jose called it the pendulum effect.

"We want the pendulum to stop," he told my friend, "we don't want it to swing to the right."

If Jose felt this way, how did the rest of the Cuban population feel about the exiles?

"No," and I told him about Jose. "Who are the fakes here, the *gusanos* or Smith and Jones?"

"Smith and Jones run into these three clowns and buy their story," Norm said, "and they see accolades, promotions, hell, medals, if they run an operation that actually topples the Communists. They do what no one else has been able to do in more than forty years. They become legends."

"And that's worth . . ."

"In the Agency," he cut me off, "that scenario would be worth everything. Life and death would be meaningless."

I didn't like having that knowledge, but realized it was the truth. With the current political climate in Washington, an operation that promised to end forty years of communism in Cuba would have priority over everything else, including the lives of a few superfluous Key Westers.

"What if the Cubans are lying to everyone?" Norm said. "What if they are going about these trips and there's nothing in Cuba, no general, no party official. What happens?"

"I don't know." I thought about it. "You think it's a scam and when it runs out, what? They're just three more Cuban exiles."

"If they pull the scam off," he said, "and then come back

with their boat shot up and say the general and party guy were captured . . ."

"Or killed."

"What happens to them? They're here, have contacts, future jobs."

"And no one ever knows the truth."

"It's another angle," he said.

We sat quietly and thought about the option of the whole thing being a scam. I got angry, thinking Tom could have died because of a con.

"What do we do next?" I stood up and looked out at the harbor.

"We get some sleep." Norm checked his watch. "We have a breakfast meeting with your friends at someplace called Harpoon Harry's, at nine."

It was almost three in the morning.

"Why?"

"Because we planned it last night." He joined me by the patio door and opened it.

We watched the small lights on boats moored by Christmas Tree Island bob in the rough harbor water. A few lone stars poked into the black night as the clouds cleared.

"Maybe one of your friends has a fresh idea," Norm said. "And we need to eat, so why not breakfast?"

We smelled as damp as the outside air felt.

"You did a good job at the cemetery," he said. "I wasn't sure you could handle it, after all this time."

"I wasn't either," I said. "I'm still shaking."

"It's cold in here." He smiled and closed the sliding glass door. "Check on Tita, she's the most fragile, right now."

TWENTY-EIGHT

Sunlight forced its way past the half-closed curtains and filled the room, waking me at 7 a.m. Tita lay beside me, hugging a pillow. I wanted to go back to sleep, but knew I couldn't. I stared at the back of her head, her midnight-black hair fell loosely down bare shoulders, and I wondered where she was in her dreams. I got out of bed quietly, slipped my damp shorts on, and left her sleeping.

Norm sat at the table with a fresh pot of coffee. He looked showered and wore his shirt hanging over his jeans, hiding his gun. He nodded hello and rolled a syringe on the table with his palm. I poured myself a cup of coffee and added two sugars.

"Doctor Feel Good?" I sat down. "You still use that stuff?"

"I'm too old to get by on three hours sleep," he drawled and returned to rolling the syringe. "Vitamins, you don't use them anymore?" He smiled.

Norm often goes without sleep for days, when he's on assignment. I had witnessed him work a string of stressful days with only an hour or two of rest, and one morning I walked in on him as he was injecting himself in the butt. First, I thought he was diabetic, but he explained it was an agency-supplied vitamin with lots of B12. I think it had a little more amphetamine in it than B12, but it worked and I wasn't about to lecture him. He had taught me to inject myself long ago and I had forgotten all about it, until then. As unhealthy and dangerous as it was, sometimes it was what it took to get the job done. I never really believed his agency supplied it, but I knew he had many shady doctors as contacts, and they would have.

"I swallow my vitamins now." I said. "What time is breakfast?"

"Nine." He freshened his coffee. "How's Tita?"

"Sleeping. I'm surprised she can sleep."

"Maybe she's stronger than you think."

"Maybe." I looked out at the clear blue sky and sparkling harbor and it was hard to remember how frightening last night had been. "A new day. What's it hold for us?"

"Doug called about a half hour ago." He refilled his cup. "The Cubans set out this morning on the go-fast," he said flatly and didn't even break a smile.

I looked at him, expecting a laugh or an explanation, but I got nothing, just the blank stare he had when he said it and hunched shoulders.

"What the hell are you talking about?" I waited for something.

"Doug called and said they took off, what don't you understand?" He drank his coffee.

"Why are we sitting here doing nothing?"

"You gonna chase 'em down with the *Fenian Bastard*?" He almost smiled. "What does she do, six knots, right?"

"We have to do something," I said.

"I've done something, but it ain't much." He continued to drink his coffee, leaving enough of a gap in our conversation to make me anxious.

"What have you done?"

"Friday night, Doug and I went to the marina," he said. "Remember all the rain? Of course, you do, that's all it seems to do in the evenings, rain. Anyway, we poured about a gallon of rain water in each of their fuel tanks." A small grin spread across his face. "Doug thought they might make the reef before the engines fouled. They'll need help. Who do they call?"

"Perkins at Tow Boat US," I said. "They can reach him on

channel 16."

"Or they call Smith and Jones." His face had a sour expression on it. "Damn it, I wish I knew their real names and who they were with."

"What are we going to do?"

"Doug is monitoring channel 16, and when their call for help comes in, he'll call me." He finished his coffee. "Now, the questions is, what are we gonna do?"

He waited for me to say something, but I was stumped because I wanted him to have the answer.

"Will the Police Chief arrest them, if we let him know?" He got tired of waiting for my reply.

"He said he would." My expression must have said more.

"But what?"

"He told me the Feds could get them out, claim jurisdiction, something like that."

"No doubt about that." He stood and opened the patio door. A cool breeze blew a hint of freshness into the stale room. "The Feds take them and they get lost in the maze and you never hear about them again. Maybe they're still able to go forward with the operation, but you would lose 'em."

"We could rent a boat at Garrison Bight and go after them." I was grabbing at straws and we both knew it. "We know they're going to breakdown."

"That's what I would do, if I had four or five more trained men available." He walked to the patio. "You and I wouldn't have a chance, even if we used two boats. Any of your friends do military duty?"

"No!" I shouted and went out with him. "No way are we gonna use them in something like this."

"I'm open to ideas." He faced me and his expression said he wasn't playing now.

"I can't put them in that position. They'd do it, but . . ." I shook my head.

"Do you think they're going to Cuba, for whatever reason?"

"There has to be some truth in their story, no matter how small. I was thinking about Smith and Jones, they contacted Richard Dowley after he ran a check on the three Cubans, so, if they aren't Feds, they have ties, strong ones, with some agency."

"I've thought about it, too." He leaned against the railing. "If, and it's a big if, but if the operation is really about bringing out a general and communist party official, with the idea of using them to topple the Cuban government, everything is possible." Norm's face hardened, because he could have been talking about himself. "Like I explained to Tita last night, innocent people die in war and anything to do with Cuba is war, just like Castro was still there. Things can be forgiven, Mick. Some boat bum, a journalist, an attorney, hell, a half dozen more could die and it would all be swept away if the operation was successful."

We watched a couple of charter boats head out of the harbor, glad to have the sunshine and westerly winds. The Gulf Stream would be popular with boaters this weekend, commercial and private vessels, all enjoying the flat water and good fishing.

"It kind of limits our choices."

"What choices?" he asked.

"I could write about it, expose the murders."

"Include it with the Kennedy conspiracy theories. What agency are they with, what are their real names and who are the Cubans, really? And if the operation works, no one in this country will care," he smiled. "I'm sorry, some liberals might care, but not anyone that counts. What other choice is there?"

The thought had come into my head earlier, but I tried to ignore it. It wouldn't go away. Would it be treason? Would it be something the Cuban people could never forgive me for doing? If I pulled it off, and I was discovered responsible, not even Norm could keep me alive. I realized, as these thoughts ran through my tired head, that I had lost all faith in my government. I had questioned it for years, no matter who lived in the White House, but now it went beyond that. Smith and Jones were the government and if they did something wrong, it was okay, as long as it served a bigger purpose. That wasn't what I expected from my government.

"If Doug hears the call, have him call Reef on his satellite phone and ask him to take as much time as possible to get the engines running. He's going to have to drain the fuel, and he shouldn't do that on the water." I didn't answer Norm's question.

"And this delay is getting us what?" He was curious.

"If they can't make their destination today, maybe they will put it off for a day, contact the people on the Cuban side, tell them one more day," I said. "I wouldn't think there's a big window for them to do this. Get in, get out."

"Okay, I agree," he stared at me, puzzled. "What's that get us?"

"It gets us nothing." I looked out at the harbor and felt the breeze. "But it gives me time to fly to Havana."

"And what?" Norm walked next to me. "What can you do in Havana?"

"Turn them over to the Cubans," I said, and wasn't sure what to feel.

"Are you crazy? You're gonna assist the Cuban government?" He stared hard and his expression showed me how concerned he was. "Who are you going to? Why would they believe you? Mick, you could end up in a Cuban jail and I can't help you there. If this is really an Agency operation, you would be committing treason."

"Treason," I yelled. "You want to talk about treason? How about treason against the people by the government? Doesn't the government have a responsibility to the people? Do you

188

think most people in this country would believe what is happening here?"

"No and that's my point," he almost yelled in reply. "The government will keep the facts hidden, so you have no real argument against them."

"And that's okay?"

"I don't know," he mumbled, "but that's the way it is and you ain't gonna change it by going to Cuba."

"So I let them get away with murder? Three murders."

"It may come to that, yes, but we can keep trying to do something, or you could be in a lot of trouble. These guys don't forgive, Mick."

"I can get the afternoon flight from Miami to Havana." I checked my watch. "But I need to get going." I ignored his concern and warning.

"You can't just fly to Havana."

"Yes I can, I have journalist credentials and one of the charter companies owes me for a feature I did on them last year."

I went inside and stopped at the table. "I need you to do a couple of things for me." I picked up the syringe. "Don't tell Tita where I've gone. Don't tell anyone and keep her safe."

"I'll do what I can, Mick, but I can't help you over there. I wish you'd listen to me. What about Bob and Burt?"

"You don't know where I went. I'll e-mail you my contact info in Havana, probably from the Hotel Nacional."

"Anything else?" He didn't look happy.

"Yeah, can I get a vitamin shot?"

TWENTY-NINE

I expected Norm to argue more than he did about my going to Havana. It wasn't like him to give in so easily, so I wanted to get going, before he was able to pull some black magic, turn this around, and stop me. I had to believe in my idea of justice and hold responsible those in the government for being forced to find justice outside our corrupted system.

I was still running off the adrenalin rush from the cemetery and felt I had to do something, if not for Tom's murder, then for what Tita and I had gone through. I have written about injustice, death squads, and corruption in Central America and I found it impossible to accept the same situations in my backyard without doing something. Norm was right, I couldn't produce any evidence to support my accusations, and it would be near impossible to get the American public, or media, to believe a federal agency was involved in a conspiracy that ignored murder and mayhem. I would probably find support from the conspiracy theorists, but few others. If I was successful, and stopped the *gusanos,* I knew Smith and Jones could easily convince the law, and the public, that I had committed treason. It didn't seem fair, but life has never guaranteed fairness.

I had to do something and that something was in Havana.

If the water-fouled fuel stopped the three Cubans, and sent them for help, I might have a half-day advantage, if they had a backup boat, I was a half day behind.

Norm, after promising to keep Tita safe, called Mike Sweet and he drove me to the marina and waited while I packed for a week. I exchanged my Glock and extra clips for two thousand dollars I hoped would cover expenses.

Things we take for granted, like deodorant and shampoo, are not readily available in Cuba. I packed extra, so I could offer them as incentives when negotiating with Cubans. I called Juan Chavez, my friend from the charter airline that made daily trips to Havana, and he held a seat for me on the 2 p.m. flight from Miami. I e-mailed my Cuban taxi-driver friend Eddie Machado and asked him to meet me at the airport; I booked a room at the Hotel Nacional on the Internet and then e-mailed Comodoro Miguel Diaz, director of the Havana Yacht Club at Marina Hemingway.

Juan's charter business once arranged educational and cultural travel packages to Cuba for Americans, but the Administration had canceled most of these licenses. American politicians and diplomats fly regularly to Havana on the charter flights.

American diplomats staff the large, old American Embassy, located along the waterfront on the Malecon, in Havana. The childish game of American diplomats being in Cuba under the Swiss flag is as big a joke as the Cuban diplomats being in Washington under the Swiss flag is. What the world has is two bullies facing off, more afraid of dialogue than blood.

As a journalist, I am able to fly to Havana without restrictions, but the Administration continues to search for opportunities to make it difficult for the independent media. Recent actions by the Justice Department, White House and Congress, leave me seriously doubting whether anyone there had read, or understands, our Constitution, or cares.

Mike Sweet dropped me at Cape Air, where I was able to get a seat on its last morning flight to Fort Lauderdale, because there were no seats available on the morning flights to Miami. I had to take a taxi to Miami International from Fort Lauderdale.

Juan had a first-class ticket waiting for me and I sat across from an American diplomat and his wife. The plane was full and took off on time. The flight itself always amazed me. By the time the jet reaches altitude, and the pilot tells passengers that Key West is visible off the left side of the plane, the decent to Jose Marti International Airport outside Havana begins. To me, the plane doesn't fly, it takes off, and then it lands. I had to fly more than one hundred and fifty miles north of Key West, so I could fly to Havana, only ninety miles south of Key West.

After the plane landed, the Cuban passengers broke out in applause, not because they were glad to be home, but because they were happy to have landed safely. It's a ceremony left over from the decades of flying Russian built airplanes. I disembarked by walking down stairs to the tarmac and followed a guide to the one-story terminal. Baggage unloading equipment moved lazily toward the plane. The weather was similar to Key West's and the sky, peppered with balls of fluffy white clouds, was the same sky I looked up at from the *Fenian Bastard* before leaving a few hours ago. The *Jose Marti—La Habana* sign on the terminal was the only indication that I was no longer in Key West.

The Immigration terminal is a large hall with a dozen enclosed booths. I lost sight of the American diplomat and his wife and wondered how the Cuban government treated them. I waited in line and when it was my turn, I handed over my passport.

"*Señor* Murphy, what brings you to Cuba?" the dark-skinned female immigration inspector asked me, as she entered my passport number into an old-fashioned computer.

"A short vacation," I lied.

"Is this your first visit?" her English was heavily accented, and her smile seemed genuine.

I knew she was looking at a computer screen that indicated how many times I had entered the island and that I'm a journalist.

"No, I've visited often for work, but now I want to see the island as a tourist."

"Where will you be staying?" Her smile remained as she slipped a stamped piece of paper into my passport.

Cubans do not stamp American passports; instead, they attach a stamped entry visa that has to be returned when the visitor leaves. This benefits the many Americans who visit the island illegally from Mexico, Canada, and Caribbean islands. When Americans who visited Cuba illegally return home, via the third country, there is no indication to American Immigrations of a stopover in Cuba, because the passport is unstamped. The passport game is as silly as using the Swiss Embassy for diplomatic purposes.

"I have reservations at the Nacional." I smiled back at her and accepted my passport.

"Please enjoy your vacation," she said and signaled the next person to come forward. Somewhere during the short conversation, she had notified Cuban Customs agents that an American journalist was coming.

I walked through the door and entered the cavernous luggage terminal. There were no luggage turntables with circling baggage. Everything had been hand placed on the floor. Soldiers walked bomb-sniffing dogs through the luggage. The Cuban government welcomes American travelers, even exiles who bring money for relatives, but they do not do it foolishly.

Customs checkout counters line up across from the terminal's glass exit doors. Armed soldiers leisurely guarded the doors. People found their luggage and many walked out without a problem from Customs. I knew from my past flights that as a journalist—on a vacation or not—my bag would be checked. I found the bag, walked toward a checkout counter, and as I did one uniformed Customs' inspector pointed. I followed, put my bag on the countertop, and opened it.

He smiled. "You have done this before." He began to pull items out of the bag.

"Yes, I'm a journalist and know you're required to check everything." I helped empty the bag.

"I apologize for the inconvenience," he scanned the clothing and toiletries. "Nothing to declare?"

"No sir, this is a short vacation, not work."

"You have a lot of shampoo and deodorants," he said and allowed me to repack my bag.

"My friends at the Cuban press office tell me their wives and girlfriends appreciate the shampoo." I put everything inside and zipped the bag. I knew that if I offered the inspector a shampoo or deodorant I would be arrested for bribery, so I only smiled my thanks.

"Enjoy your vacation." He walked back toward the other inspectors.

The automatic doors opened and outside, behind a chain-link fence, people waited for family and friends. A soldier opened the gate for me and I pushed through the people and found Eddie Machado leaning against his taxi, dressed in a shirt and tie smoking a harsh Cuban cigarette. Eddie is a Cuban entrepreneur and if capitalism ever makes its way back to the island, I expect he will be one of the first millionaires. He and his wife speak fluent English. He left the University of Havana, where he taught economics, after saving enough money by moonlighting on his days off, to buy an old Chevy taxi. He has a steady clientele of English, Canadian and American visitors and all this by word-of-mouth. By having an ample supply of American dollars, Eddie has been able to invest in a number of smaller ventures, such as copying music CD recordings for resale, *paledars*—small, family-owned restaurants the government allows residents to operate from their homes—and black-market cigar distribution that offers real Cuban cigars for a sixty-percent discount from government stores.

A university professor earns about twenty dollars a month. Eddie, as a taxi driver-entrepreneur, earns fifty dollars a day, and adds to that whatever he profits from his other investments. Of course, he is more than a taxi driver, he is a tour guide, knows where to shop and eat and can find just about anything a visitor to Havana wants, so he's well worth his daily rate.

Eddie waved when he saw me and took my bag.

"I'm sorry for the short notice." I got into the backseat. I would have sat in front, but he said on my first visit, it was better that the trip looks like business to prying eyes.

"Hey, no problem." He got in and began to drive off. "With all the new restrictions, there are not so many Americans as before, business has been slow." The restrictions were American, not Cuban.

"The Nacional, Eddie, then somewhere to eat, I'm starving." I sat back in the old Chevy Impala, the windows open to let the cool Cuban air circulate. "How is the family?"

"Everyone is healthy and busy." He stretched his arm over the seat and handed me a cigar. "I have some boxes at home for you."

He keeps a cigar cutter and matches in the ashtray. I prepared the cigar and lit it. We drove through residential neighborhoods of old apartment buildings badly in need of repair and paint, windows wide open and laundry drying on balconies, and past the railroad yards into Havana. The seawall along the Malecon was busy with people socializing, maybe some looking north and praying.

Traffic pushed its way along the old, worn, four-lane street. It was a mixture of taxis, scruffy Russian Ladas, new Korean flat-bed trucks, old buses belching smoke and "camels"—what the Cubans called the drop-frame semi tractor-trailers used to haul people around the island. Enclosed like a bus, with seats and windows, the forty-foot truck bed drops down in the center, leaving two humps, one at each end.

Eddie turned onto Calle Twenty-one and drove up the hill to the Hotel Nacional, an eight-story resort with 457 rooms, which was built in the 1930s; its elegant lobby is large, with high ceilings, and its hilltop location allowed an awesome view of the Gulf of Mexico from manicured lawns. I left my cigar in the ashtray, took my bag, and got out. Eddie waited. The doorman took my bag and handed it to a bellhop, everyone worked in Cuba.

The hotel has been host to the famous and infamous, from Hollywood's elite like Errol Flynn and Eva Gardner, to gangster Al Capone, along with Mafia bosses and sports legends of the 1950s. Meyer Lansky once had an interest in businesses within the hotel. The Nacional wears its age with pride and dignity. Every amenity is available at the hotel and it has always been one of my favorite places to stay. The grounds hold a Cuban-missile-crisis museum where the government had built shelters and bunkers, preparing for an American invasion in the 1960s.

"El Aljibe," I said as I got back into the taxi.

"You must be hungry, Mick." Eddie started the taxi and headed toward Miramar, it was on the way to Marina Hemingway and my afternoon meeting with Comodoro Miguel Diaz.

For fifteen dollars each, we got to choose from roast pollo con mojo—chicken—fish, or a combination plate of meat, chicken, rice, beans, salad and dessert. The portions were generous and tasty.

During lunch, we talked a little about Key West and a lot about life in Cuba. The large, thatched-roof restaurant is located in a residential neighborhood. I kept the reason for my visit to myself. Journalists are often followed and if Eddie was questioned, he would not have much to tell them.

"Eddie, do you have something to do after dropping me off at Marina Hemingway?" We were finishing up with Cuban coffee.

"I can wait."

"I don't think you should, this may require my being with the comodoro for a few hours." I wanted to distance my friend from whatever trouble I was facing.

THIRTY

Calle Twenty-three begins at the Malecon, climbs through the large parks and hills of residential Havana, zigzags at the Plaza de la Revolucion, becomes Calle Forty-seven on the other side of the plaza, crosses over a stream, turns into Calle Forty-two and takes you through Miramar to the Gulf. Green parks and walkways were everywhere and the mixed aroma of cut grass and tropical flowers came through the open windows. We passed the monument of the Plaza and Eddie told me about the New Year's rally that was held there, to celebrate the 1959 revolutionary victory. A large character of Che Guevara stared down from one of the plaza's buildings.

Eddie turned onto Avenida *Uno* in Miramar that followed the Gulf and I saw more than a dozen new high-rise hotels and apartments going up on the beaches. He drove down Calle Seventy, with its modest homes, many in need of paint, and turned right on Avenida Five. The avenue is wide, with spacious islands of green grass and old trees separating the four lanes, and has traffic circles controlled by police officers. Small, tree-shaded parks dotted the route. Palatial homes lined the avenue and side streets. Many of the gated homes had signs letting those passing by know the property belonged to foreign embassies. Somewhere, I had read American diplomats lived in this area.

"I can visit some friends by the marina," Eddie said as I stared at the scenery.

The roads were dusty and in need of repair, but they were busy and the sidewalks bustled with people coming and going, waiting at bus stops or eating a *frita*—a small, round Cuban bun with seasoned meat, shredded potatoes and cheese—at sidewalk stands. Children in clean school uniforms walked along, holding hands, on an outing to a park or museum.

"Do you still have your cell phone?" I watched people interact as they waited for a bus or to cross the street.

"Yes." I saw his smile in the rearview mirror. "As long as I have dollars, I can keep it."

The fortunate Cuban has dollars, whether they earned them as Eddie did, or relatives sent the allowed monthly stipend. The restrictions on sending money to Cuba came from the Americans. If you lived on pesos, you lived frugally, with ration cards and government subsidies. If you had dollars, you were able to exchange them for the new Cuban peso, after paying a ten-percent tax. The new peso allowed you to buy overpriced goods, but your cupboards were full and you had eggs, rice, real coffee, not rationed coffee that was mixed with other types of beans; you could also buy sugar and chicken all month. Cubans living on ration cards received less than a dozen eggs a month; rationed portions tended to be small.

"If you don't hear from me in a couple of hours, go home," I said, "and I'll call you from the hotel."

"I have plenty to do." He turned into the entrance of Marina Hemingway.

Eddie stopped at the guard gate and security allowed him to drive me to the yacht club. I had a feeling he knew the guards, because he did a lot of business with American boaters and I am sure dollars changed hands on a street corner somewhere.

Marina Hemingway has four man-made channels cut into the land that held seawalls for mooring boats and access roads. Hotels, restaurants, port offices, ship's store, a market, and slips take up the land and channels.

Club Nautico, the comodoro's yacht club, a two-story building that faced the water between the first and second access roads, had people coming and going. Eddie pulled up and let me out.

"Call me, I will be close," and he drove away.

I walked in the front door and through the open sliding glass door saw the channel and boats tied off to the seawall. A circular stairway stood in the center of the room. A comfortable clubroom was to the left of the stairway and a busy bar filled the room to the right. I didn't see Miguel, so I climbed the stairs to his office. I knocked on his door.

"*Entrar,*" came from behind the closed door. I walked in.

His white-walled office is large and bright from window light. A dark wooden desk sits in the center of the room, a couch against a wall and two leather directors' chairs in front of his desk. Comodoro Miguel Diaz dressed in his white pants and blue nautical shirt, his usual uniform, stood and extended his hand.

"A pleasure my friend." We shook hands and he came around to the front of the desk and hugged me—*abrazo,* a Latin show of friendship. His bushy white hair always looked in need of cutting. "You fly, so this is business." He returned to his seat.

"Not my normal business," I said. "I need some advice and, possibly, your help."

"Of course," he smiled, but I saw concern in his eyes. "Whatever I can do to help a friend."

I told him the whole story, starting with Tom's murder and ending with the shootings at the cemetery. I wondered if he knew Tom, and guessed he would have because of all of Tom's visits to the marina. I avoided mentioning Norm, otherwise I told him the truth. When I referred to the three Cuban deserters, he looked uncomfortable, but allowed me to continue without interruption.

He sat quietly after I finished and ran his hands through his hair. "You brought copies of the photos?"

"Of course. As I said, only two of the men are photographed and I doubt the names are their real ones."

"You think they are here, at Marina Hemingway?"

"If they left today, yes."

"With the westerly winds, timing would be important, especially if they were in a hurry to get out of Cuban jurisdiction and back into international waters with their passengers."

"My thoughts, exactly."

Miguel stood up and opened the glass doors to the second-floor balcony. He took a cigar out of his pocket, cut the end, and lit it. He pointed to the box on his desk and I helped myself to one of his cigars. I used the desk cutter and lighter.

"What is it you want me to do?" He had his back to me and stared out at the water.

"Help me track them down and turn them in to the right authorities." I joined him on the balcony.

He turned to me and the smile was gone. He took the cigar out of his mouth and rolled it between his fingers. "I like you, Mick. I like all the American sailors who come here, but what you are asking is a delicate matter. I can easily find out if they have arrived here, even at other marinas." He puffed on the cigar. "The next step is the sensitive one. Do I go to the Havana police?" He looked at me.

"What are the other options?"

"You tell an amazing story, and I believe you, or at least I believe these are the things you have been told. But you come here as an American with promises of turning in three Cuban army deserters who are working for your, what, CIA?"

"I told you, I don't know what agency, only that the Police Chief told me they were agents for federal officers." I looked out and saw people at the Hotel Acuario pool.

An afternoon breeze picked up and cooled the air, not unlike what was probably happening in Key West at the same time. I was suddenly tired and wondered if Norm's vitamin shot had worn off.

"But these men were soldiers," he bit down on the end of the cigar, "so that would involve the *Fuerza Armada Revolucianlaries*, or because of their plan to help others leave the island illegally, maybe I would need to notify the *Estado de la Segurida*."

I understood his dilemma. He held a prominent position within the Cuban boating community, and it was a small world. He traveled freely to the United States and Europe, expounding the boating virtues of Cuba and its waters. He might have met, he might even know officials from the various police agencies socially, but he would not want a working relationship with them. To breach his friendships with these officials, especially for an American that he could never be truly sure was not a CIA agent, was asking for the impossible.

"But, first," his smile returned as he smoked the cigar, "let us see if they are here, before we do anything else."

He closed the glass door, picked up the phone, and dialed. In rapid Spanish, he asked if any go-fast boats from the United States arrived that afternoon.

"Three," he hung up the phone, "arrived since noon. I did not ask about the people on it, I thought we could walk around and see, first."

"Thank you." I puffed on the cigar and followed him out of the office and down the stairs.

Like any marina in the late afternoon, boaters and workers sat around enjoying the weather and a drink. The talk was loud, about fish that got away and the women they would dance with later. Others complained about needed repairs, while some grumbled about having to leave tomorrow. It didn't matter the language, I knew what they were saying.

We followed the road to the last finger of land and walked to the port office. We talked about the weather, and how, because of politics, the Conch Republic Sailboat Race would not take place. All varieties of boats were tied off, many with Canadian, British, French and Mexican cities painted below the boats' names. Those that flew only the courtesy Cuban flag, I assumed were American. American military satellites can pinpoint boats at the marina and looked for the Stars and Strips.

"Boaters have no politics." He smoked the last of his cigar. "The seas have no borders."

"We might still come," I said, but didn't believe it. "Maybe things will change in a few months."

"That would be nice," he smiled, and I didn't think he believed it, either.

The harbormaster's office was halfway down the road in a single-story building. The main room held six desks with computers and boaters were questioning the employees about tomorrow's weather. I was surprised to see so many Americans. Miguel walked into the harbormaster's office. He introduced me to Moses Torres.

"Mick is looking for a couple of friends from Key West," Miguel explained and I handed him the photo of Lu and the two Cubans. "They should have come in this afternoon."

"This one," Moses pointed to the man on Lu's right, "came in a little while ago, and signed papers. He's Cuban," he looked at Miguel with a quizzical look. "He and his friends come regularly." He gave me back the photo. From his desk, he took a clipboard and flipped some pages. "Their boat is in slip twenty-two, by the yacht club."

"Thank you." I turned to Miguel, "I must have just missed them."

"Yes," Moses said. "He asked if I had seen a taxi driver they know. I told him no, so he went looking for him."

"What driver?" Miguel asked.

"Enrique Garcia." Moses still had the puzzled expression. "He retired from the military, you know him, Miguel."

"A big man, balding and with a mustache, right?"

"Yes," and he put the clipboard back on his desk.

We thanked him and walked out. It was getting dark.

"Now do you believe me?" We walked back toward the yacht club.

"I believed you before." He slowed down and looked toward the Gulf. "My problem is I am not sure how to help you." He put his arm around my shoulder and we continued to walk. "But something must be done."

THIRTY-ONE

Miguel and I stopped at the *Chan-Chan* restaurant and drank Cuban rum while the sun set west of Havana. The outdoor bar was crowded with a mixture of foreign boaters and Cuban workers, celebrating the end of another day. Miguel's contention that boaters didn't have politics may not have been entirely true, but it was generally correct. In Key West, there was little talk of politics, especially national politics, unless it somehow affected what we did on the water. Fishermen had their gripes with state and federal regulations that cost them fish, but did not affect foreign fishing boats; and sailors had complaints when bureaucrats in Washington established imaginary borders on our waterways. Otherwise, it didn't matter a sailor's nationality, sex or sexual preference, or political persuasion at the end of the day, only that he or she enjoyed the sunset and a cold drink.

"If you have things to discuss we should do it here." Miguel sipped his rum and Coke. "My office is not the best place to talk."

I was confused for a minute and then understood that he meant there was a bug in his office and I appreciated the warning. It was a sign that he trusted me, or was concerned about what I might say and involve him. I lit the stub of the cigar I started in his office.

"I understand." I puffed on the cigar and saw he was trying very hard to keep a smile. "I think I've told you everything that brought me here."

Miguel was trying to read my expression, to see if I understood that someone, somewhere, had already heard everything I had told him earlier. He was giving me time to make an escape. I ordered us two more drinks from the petite Cuban waitress.

"I could get security and arrest them at their boat." He sipped the new drink. "Turn them over to the local police and you can tell your story. If they are three deserters, they will be identifiable."

I didn't think that was what he wanted to do. If a general and party official were involved in the plot, it would be important to the Cubans to get them all. Miguel might have been playing it safe, because he could control the marina's security force and if the initial check cleared the three Cubans, it would go no further.

"I'll leave that decision to you." I stubbed out the end of my cigar. "I think we should check out their boat."

"Yes, I agree," he finished his drink, "but from my office because they know you."

"Good point." I finished my drink. "Should we go?"

"Yes."

The sun had set and the early winter darkness blanketed the marina. Boat lights highlighted the docks and grass patches along the slips. Across from one channel, the windows from the condominiums splashed light onto the waterway and salsa music flowed from the complex. Night blossoming jasmine brought a pleasant aroma to the evening and a full moon added soft light to the marina.

The yacht club's bar was full. People gathered there to meet before heading to Havana or a local restaurant. Men chose the bar, while their wives readied themselves at the marina's showers or finished dressing at the boat. The talk was lively and the single bartender kept busy pouring Havana Club Rum or opening bottles of Crystal beer.

Pressed pants, deck shoes without socks and colorful tropical shirts, replaced cutoff jeans and T-shirts from the afternoon.

Miguel pointed to his office and while I walked the stairway, he greeted the men and women in the bar.

I found a wall switch and turned on the office lights. I looked out the patio door and tried to find slip twenty-two. Even numbered slips would be on my right. I guessed that the boat slip would be halfway along the seawall. All the boats had light coming from within.

Miguel came in and went to his desk for a pair of binoculars. He gave them to me. "On the right."

"I know." I opened the sliding glass door and went outside. I adjusted the glasses and found slip twenty-two. The large numbers were old and faded. The boat was about thirty feet long and dull light showed from one forward porthole. I scanned the area around the boat and saw nothing. Many of the other boats had lawn chairs set up, even a few barbecues, but nothing was on the lawn outside the go-fast in slip twenty-two.

"I asked in the bar about the boat." Miguel sat at his desk. "Three men came in around two this afternoon, tied off, and left in a taxi about the time you came in."

I scanned the area one more time and returned the binoculars to him. I sat down.

"Is there someplace I could show up and tell my story?" My adrenalin was pumping, now that I knew for sure they were here.

"Of course," he grinned. "We have, *come se dice*," he thought of what he wanted to say, "hospitals for the mental." He grinned broadly, proud of his joke.

"You don't think I would be believed." I ignored his attempt at humor.

"In time." He looked concerned, the grin lost, and I wondered if it was for himself or me. "But if they plan to get their passengers and make a run for it, you don't have time."

We sat without talking and a cool breeze blew in the open door.

"I have a friend in the Havana police, a detective," he stared over my head, "that I can meet for drinks and maybe he will listen."

I wondered if he was avoiding eye contact or indicating where the listening bug was. It didn't matter.

"We don't have time to waste, Miguel."

He picked up his desk phone and dialed. He asked to talk with Capitán Jorge Torres and waited for a couple of minutes before he talked again. Miguel asked the captain to meet him at El Gato Tuerto—One-Eyed Cat—located a block from the Hotel Nacional and the Malecon.

"This detective speaks English and I have known him for a long time." Miguel nervously twisted in his seat. "I do not guarantee anything."

"It's more than I could do on my own, I appreciate it."

"He may do nothing, he may arrest you, hell, he may arrest me. too," he forced a smile. "But he is a place to begin, to see what he thinks."

Miguel parked his two-year-old Toyota at the Hotel Nacional and we walked down the small hill to Calle zero y nineteen, to El Gato. The steep sidewalk was in need of repair and we walked around large cracks, sometimes stepping into the street. I had a good view of the Malecon with vehicles of all sorts zipping along, as we walked. The hum of traffic was louder than that along North Roosevelt Boulevard by Garrison Bight Marina during Fantasy Fest week, Key West's answer to Mardi Gras. The side streets were crowded with parked cars, scooters, and motorcycles. A high-rise building stood off at the end of the street, across from the Malecon, and most of its windows were lit, while the smaller buildings along the street were dark and seemed deserted.

"Have you been to El Gato before?" Miguel walked carefully around a large crack in the street.

"Yes." I walked around the crack. "I've been there a few times."

Taxis parked outside the popular club waited for customers, while people gathered on the steps, talking or waiting for friends, and others came and went. A large pond filled with color from underwater lights took up the front entrance of the club and a small footbridge led across it to a large, solid Spanish-designed wood wall. The wall was actually the door to the club. A doorman rotated the whole wall inward for us to enter.

We were greeted by a maître d' in the crowded lobby. Miguel whispered to him and he walked into the club. Small tables for two in the vestibule were occupied. A trio was playing American songs from the 50s on stage. The maître d' waved us forward and we followed him down a few steps into the main room which was crowded and dark. A large bar took up a third of the room and all the seats held patrons. Off past the bar we walked up two steps to a section filled with large tables. The maître d' pointed to one table that a single man sat at and walked away.

Miguel introduced me to Capitán Jorge Torres of the Havana Police Department. We shook hands and I saw a resemblance to Key West Police Detective Luis Morales and wasn't sure if that was a good sign. Jorge had the good looks of Luis, but a few more years and a little more gray in the hair. His mustache was thick and well groomed. He wore a pale yellow *guayabera* shirt. I had to force myself to stop staring.

"Is something wrong?" Jorge frowned at my stare.

"I'm sorry," and I sat down next to Miguel. "You remind me of a policeman in Key West."

We ordered three rum and Cokes with limes.

"And what is his name, Luis Morales?" he smiled.

Nothing could have been more surprising to me. I must have shown my shock.

"Luis' mother and my mother are sisters," Jorge sipped his drink and explained the likeness.

"How do you know about Luis?" I sucked a piece of ice from my drink.

"Our mothers keep in touch," he said. "Luis refuses to visit." When he said this, his hand cupped his chin and stroked it, as if he had a beard. This was the way Cubans discussed Fidel Castro's Cuba when they didn't want to speak about it. What he was saying, and I understood, as did Miguel, was that Luis wouldn't return to Cuba while it was ruled by Communist Fidelistas.

"I don't know his family." I chewed the ice. "But Luis is involved in what brings me here."

Jorge tapped the seat next to him and I moved there. The seat gave him a full view of the club and his back was to the wall.

"You have police business to discuss?" He looked suspiciously at Miguel. "My office would have been better."

"He needs advice first," Miguel said. "I thought, because of your English, you would be the person to talk to. Jorge has worked with American law enforcement before."

"The highway murders?" I guessed.

"Yes," he seemed surprised. "You know of that in America?"

"The Cuban police and FBI worked together to solve it."

"Havana Police," he corrected me. "Are you with the FBI?" For a moment he seemed confused, but a shake of Miguel's head changed that.

"I need to tell you some things that have happened to me in the last ten days," I said, "and that will explain why I'm here."

He lit a cigarette and sat back in his chair. When he sat there quietly, I took it to mean for me to begin. I repeated my tale for the second time in only a few hours. He listened intently, his eyes darting often between Miguel and me. By the time I finished, he had chain-smoked five Cuban cigarettes and finished his drink. I wished Eddie had given me a box of cigars.

"Interesting," he looked at Miguel. "Are you a communist?" He turned his look to me.

"No, why?"

"Most Americans would like to see . . ." he stroked his chin again, "the Communists gone, am I not right?"

It was going to get sticky and I knew I would have to choose my words carefully. "I cannot speak for most Americans, Jorge. But, for me, this is not about politics it's about justice. Justice for the murder of my friend and two young girls I didn't even know."

He thought for a minute before speaking. "But the two girls died because of you."

"How's that?"

"Well, you said you pointed out the wrong boat to one of the men and that they killed the girls and started the fire to get back at you."

"That's what I believe. How does that make me responsible for the girls' deaths?"

"Semantics, I guess." He stared with the brown eyes of a hardened cop. "However, your authorities condone these murders and you have come to Havana for justice. Why do you think you will find justice here?" He sipped melted ice water from his empty rum and Coke.

"The Key West police don't condone what these men have done, but federal agents have interfered with them doing anything," I said and took a drink. "Because these men are deserters from the Cuban Army, I thought Cuban authorities would want to apprehend them."

"I am sure that is right." He lit another cigarette. "But authority may be a problem."

"I have mentioned state security and military police," Miguel said.

"Are you involved, Miguel, because they have a boat at the marina?" Jorge turned to Miguel.

"No," I said before Miguel could answer. "Miguel is not involved at all. He is one of the few people I know and trust in Havana, so I came to him for advice. That's all."

"If what you are saying is true, we do not have much time," he ordered more drinks, "but things do not move swiftly in Cuba. I cannot act on something like this without bringing it to superiors." He looked at his watch. "And at this hour, I am not sure I want to call them."

"You've gotta be kidding me." I almost slammed my fists on the table and it was difficult to keep my voice down. "You've got three military deserters who are trying to topple the government and it's too late to wake up your bosses?"

Jorge had a big smile for my outburst. "First, I have nothing but a story from you and you leave me no time to investigate, only act. That concerns me. Second, if you are right, I do not have the jurisdiction to make the arrest."

I sat back in my chair, drained my drink, and closed my eyes. It was beginning to appear that I was becoming responsible for justice, as Padre Thomas had suggested a few days ago.

"Do not look so discouraged." He glanced at Miguel. "Americans," and they both laughed as our new drinks arrived. "I have a friend in state security I can call. If they will talk to you, I will take you to their office and Miguel should go home."

"That's fine with me." I sat back up and took a drink. "There's no reason for Miguel to tag along."

For the first time since sitting down, I became aware of the noise of the club. Music mixed with conversations, waitresses, and bartenders yelled orders back and forth. The trio on stage sang American oldies and it seemed unreal hearing a song from the 1950s in a Cuban club.

"Excuse me, while I go outside to call." His resemblance to Luis stood out, again. He stopped before stepping down to the main room. "You are aware of the seriousness of these accusations, right?" He cupped his chin, stroked an imaginary beard, and then took a long swallow of his fresh drink. "As a courtesy to *mi primo* Luis, I warn you that state security will try to prove you are CIA. They are not trusting." He turned and walked away.

"Why is this so difficult?" I turned to Miguel.

"No trust between our governments." He sipped his drink. "Maybe, because of the timeline, they will choose to believe you first."

"That's a good thing, right?" I nervously took a long swallow of my drink.

"No," he said with a frown, "it means that they keep you in custody until all this is sorted out." He looked at his watch. "Sunrise is around 7 a.m., so there's still a lot of time. My guess is the *gusanos* leave the marina before five, then head to the rendezvous location, pick up their passengers and head north while it's dark. The full moon should be setting by then."

"That would be my plan, if I were them."

Jorge walked up to the table and handed me the bill for the drink. "Have mi primo Luis reimburse you," he joked. "Tell my cousin it was my birthday."

"Where are we going?" I paid with dollars and followed the two men out of the club.

The doorman spun the large wall for us and we walked out into the cool evening. Jorge whispered something to Miguel, who nodded.

"I will wait in my office, hoping something good happens

before they leave," he said to me and we shook hands. He walked down the steps and turned toward the Hotel Nacional.

"I will drive." Jorge pointed toward the Malecon as we walked through the people waiting outside. "It won't take long."

"I appreciate this," I said and followed him along the dark sidewalk.

"Wait until it is over, before you thank me."

Thirty-Two

Jorge drove a new unmarked KIA Havana Police Car with a domed red emergency light in the back window. He turned the police radio off as he drove slowly through the night.

"You know my cousin, you are friends?" He turned his head away from the road for a second to show me a friendly smile. He lit a cigarette and put the match in an ashtray that was overflowing with cigarette stumps, ashes and burned matchsticks.

"Not really." I wasn't sure what he wanted me to say, so I stuck to the truth. "He is against boaters who come here." I cupped my chin and stroked my beard.

Jorge laughed as I did it. "Yes, that is what I hear from family. I thought maybe they said it thinking it would make us feel better." He drove slower than any Cuban I've ever driven with did. "Is he a good policeman?"

"What is good?"

"We hear so many police in America are corrupt." He turned to me again, the cigarette dangling from his lips. "They beat and kill black men, take bribes from the Mafia, shoot unarmed minorities."

"I can assure you, Luis is not like that." I smiled to myself because I never thought I would be defending Luis. "He is a good cop and the bad cops you hear about are few and far between."

"I spent time at our embassy in London." He pulled into the

driveway of the Hotel Habana Libre and parked. "I think because my English is good I get to deal with the American FBI. They seemed surprised that I was an honest cop that cared about solving the murder." He pushed the cigarette in the ashtray.

"Jorge, you need to remember how you hear negative things about American cops, we hear the same type of rumors about Cuban cops." I turned to him. His use of the word cop told me he understood a lot. "In America, you are all the secret police that scare the populace."

"Too much misunderstanding, too many rumors," he sighed.

We got out of the car and he pointed toward the hotel entrance.

"Your office is here?" I followed him into the large lobby.

"No, but I know the bartender." He walked to the lobby's Siboney Bar.

The Hotel Habana Libre opened on March 19, 1958 as a Hilton Hotel. The 574-room hotel served as headquarters to the Cuban rebels after their December 1959 victory and was the scene of many of the new government's news conferences. Fidel Castro, and other leaders of the revolution, stayed at the hotel and the lobby has large framed black-and-white, poster-styled photographs documenting the victorious armed guerrillas lounging around.

I followed Jorge as he walked to the bar. He greeted a woman who sat alone. Her skin was the color of heavily creamed coffee and her shoulder-length hair was as black as Tita's. They shook hands as she stood. She was five-foot-ten and dressed casually in dark slacks, a green blouse, and comfortable shoes.

"Mick Murphy, please allow me to introduce Capitán Idania Ricon of the Estado de la Seguridad," Jorge introduced the attractive woman.

"My pleasure." I took her hand and had the urge to kiss it,

but she pulled it away after a mellow handshake.

Jorge ordered us rum and Cokes and we sat on a couch, away from the bar. Idania chose a large chair facing us. The front desk was at the other side of the large marble lobby and busy, but the Siboney was quiet.

"Your passport, please." She held her hand out.

I took the passport from my back pocket and handed it to her. She looked through it and in Spanish joked that Americans liked to visit the island but were afraid to have their passports stamped. *Why is it,* she asked Jorge, *Cuba scares the American government?* Jorge laughed and said, *Maybe because all the Cubans that had left were either ugly, corrupt or stupid and Americans thought we were all like that. We should talk English,* he said and she smiled at me.

"Why, Jorge," she said in English and gave me back my passport, "he understands Spanish. Why do people call you Mick if your first name is Liam?"

"I'm Irish and many Irish are called Mick." I didn't want to go into the long explanation of my nickname. She must have read my facial expressions, to know I understood Spanish. On the other hand, it might have been a good guess.

"Jorge and I were in England together," it explained her English, "and met some Irish. I liked most of them."

It wouldn't have surprised me if she had met with the IRA.

At Jorge's prompting, I told her my story. Jorge listened intently, looking for errors that would indicate I was lying, and Idania's large brown eyes never blinked. I handed her the photo of the two Cubans and Lu. She looked at it, turned it over and read the names, then she spoke into a small button-like pin on her blouse and a tall black man crossed the lobby. She walked him to the door, handed him the photo, returned, and took her same seat.

She hadn't said a word. She sipped her drink and looked at

Jorge and then me. From her purse, she took a cigarette, offered Jorge and me one, I declined, Jorge accepted, and they smoked. The lobby noise filled the silence. When she was finished with the cigarette, she put it out in an ashtray.

"You are either a very brave man or a very foolish one," her tone gave away nothing about how she was thinking. She was not afraid to stare directly at me to see my reaction to her words.

"Maybe neither, but a little of both." I took a gulp of my drink. If we had been in a police station, I would have been frightened.

"Jorge is a good policeman, I know that from our time in England and what he has done in Havana." She lit another cigarette without offering one to Jorge. "He does not fully understand what you are saying, but I do." She hesitated and sipped from her glass. "Do you, *Señor?*"

Lights from passing cars flashed across the hotel's large windows, harshly highlighting sections of the lobby, briefly. Whenever the lobby door opened, hectic sounds flooded in.

I took a deep breath in and blew it out. "If there is a general and party official secretly working together to overthrow the government, it is serious and it becomes more serious if Washington is involved."

"Jorge wasn't sure the story had any truth to it," she subbed out the cigarette, "but I know better. My brother is with the military police and he is working on locating three Army officers who disappeared about a year ago."

Jorge sat up straight. He suddenly realized he could be in the middle of something big and I wasn't sure if that made him happy or not. Primo Luis would never forgive me if I did something that hurt Primo Jorge.

"That piece of your story is keeping me here and you out of jail." She checked her watch. "A couple of years ago we discovered, with the help of your DEA, that some military offi-

cers were involved in protecting Colombian drug smugglers."
She lit another cigarette and Jorge lit one of his own. "Generales Guardia y Ochoa were tried and convicted." She left out
the part about their execution. "Some of their junior officers
were also sent to prison and some escaped. Afterward, three
officers vanished. My brother and some of his associates feel the
Colombians helped them, or executed them to keep them quiet."

"But if Mick is right, it is the Americans," Jorge said.

"The three that vanished were not connected to Guardia and
Ochoa." She finished her drink. "But military intelligence was
able to connect them to drug trafficking, later, even after we
thought we had put a stop to it. It was assumed that someone
leaked the information about their arrest and that was how they
got away." She lit a new cigarette off the burning ember of the
one she just finished. "Maybe it was the general and maybe the
drug running was a way to collect money for him and the party
official to live on in exile, or maybe they have other traitors
involved and really plan to overthrow the government."

"You know where they are, but you don't have much time if
you want to catch them." I finished my drink. "They have to be
planning to leave before sunrise."

"And you, *Señor*, tomorrow you could be a hero in Cuba."
She smiled almost honestly. "But you are only looking for
justice, is that correct?"

"Yes." I raised my empty glass. Jorge nodded and walked to
the bar. "I want to know that the men who killed my friend are
off the streets and unable to kill again." Jorge brought us all
fresh drinks. Idania's was a mojito. I took a long swallow to wet
my dry throat.

Idania looked curiously at Jorge and he shrugged his
shoulders and nodded at the same time.

"You are not so naïve as to believe these men will go to
prison." She stirred her drink and took a sip.

"You want to shoot them, good for you." I took another drink. "I'm tired of killing, I'm tired of losing friends. I guess I've depended on the Cuban government to execute them from the time I decided to come here."

The black man who had taken the photo came back into the hotel and sat at the bar. Jorge pointed so Idania turned and then got up and walked to the man. They spoke briefly and he left. She came back, sat down, and lit another cigarette. She inhaled deeply and took a drink.

"I was not joking about being a hero," she said.

"If all this goes down and I'm connected to it, I could be arrested for treason at home, and let me assure you, the agents running these men would do it to me in a heart beat." I took another swallow of my drink. It was almost gone.

"You could stay in Cuba, I can arrange that." She smiled brightly because she already knew the answer.

"Thank you, but I have friends and someone special in Key West." I knew, and so did they, because of the time they had spent in England, that I could not survive in Cuba as a journalist. It wasn't money, it was the loss of my ability to question government, and without it, I would not survive.

"Jorge and I must gather up some officers and go to Marina Hemingway." She took a stiff drink, put out her cigarette, and stood. "Do you need someone to go with you to the Nacional?"

"I would like to go with you," I said.

"You are not here," she smiled and sipped her mojito. "You are not here, for your own sake, as you have said. Go back to the Nacional. Jorge and I will take credit for this and we do not know you."

I finished the last of my drink and stood. I shook hands with both of them. "Will someone let me know in the morning how it went?"

"Of course," Jorge said.

"You know they will have American papers, maybe even citizenship," I said as we walked toward the lobby.

"The American Interests Section notifies Cubans coming from America that our government does not recognize the right of the American government to protect so-called Cuban-born American citizens. It is on their Web site, you should check it out when you return to Key West," Idania said. "So, when we get them it will not matter. Also, something like this, the Americans will not want press. We might, but they won't. You go now and Jorge and I will keep your name out of our reports. Enjoy Havana, *Señor.*" She and Jorge walked out of the hotel.

I went to the lobby gift shop and bought a Romeo and Juliet Churchill cigar. The counter sales clerk cut it and gave me matches. I lit it in the lobby. Crowds of young Cubans waited for the elevators to take them to the rooftop club so they could dance and listen to live entertainment.

It was cool outside, a full moon looked down and from the corner of Calle Twenty-three, I could see the Malecon, traffic still running along the water's edge. It was ten o'clock and I decided to walk the few blocks to the hotel. Halfway down the street, enjoying my cigar, I walked a side street, Calle N, toward Calle Twenty-one and the Hotel Capri, another old Mafia hotel from before the revolution. The hotel had a nice bar with live entertainment and it was still early for a Saturday night in Havana. I told myself not to celebrate too early, but I thought I could toast Tom with a shot of Havana Club Anejo and enjoy the rest of the cigar.

Calle N is a narrow street and it was dark for the long block to Calle Twenty-one. Cuban streets are usually safe and I felt secure walking anywhere, no matter the time. I was pleased with myself for accomplishing the impossible. In the morning, I would e-mail the news and maybe stay another day or two. I could spend the day with Eddie and his family, visit some other friends from the Cuban press and head home midweek.

I didn't notice the car as it moved up the dark street because it didn't have its lights on. I turned when I heard the doors open, but it was too late. Two men jumped out and pushed me back against the wall, I dropped my cigar. One hit me in the stomach and the punch took the air out of me. I slid down only to be kicked in the stomach and it seemed impossible to breathe. They picked me up and tossed me in the backseat of the car. I saw a man's image in my dazed vision and slid into him as I moved across the seat. The doors closed and the car sped away without anyone saying a word.

THIRTY-THREE

The man in the backseat knocked me to the floor. Breathing was difficult. I took short breaths, trying to fill my burning lungs with air. Two men sat above me, their feet holding me down, and the car moved quickly through the streets. One foot forced my head down against the floor. The old carpet smelled like grease and oil. The odor made me nauseous. The car moved too fast; I could hear the tires on the road, and at each turn, my body slid and hit against the back or front seat. I could feel a downhill motion and someone opened a window. My arms were pinned under me. I turned my head and tried to breathe through my mouth, to avoid the odor, and a foot put pressure on my neck. No one spoke. Someone turned the radio on and loud salsa music filled the car.

I listened intently for something I could recognize, I don't know why; I heard only the sounds of traffic as the car sped along. Havana nightlife didn't begin until midnight, so I thought the traffic had to be heading to Havana, which meant we were heading away from the old city. I wanted to think this was a kidnapping of a tourist, but I knew better and it frightened me. The car slowed down, and I guessed we had to be in Miramar because the car had stopped making sharp turns that suggested the narrow streets of Havana. Maybe we were past Miramar and going toward Marina Hemingway. Neither of these were good signs.

The car slowed more and made a few wide turns. Light

splashed over me, but the heavy foot held me down. The silence told me they knew where they were going and that suggested my abduction was planned. But how? I hadn't been in Havana eight hours.

I heard each time a tire hit a pothole or bump, and felt it, too. We left the paved road and I suffered as the tires rode over dirt and rocks, as the car slowed down. The light stopped flashing above me, and the floor became pitch black. We stopped and I heard a door open, but could not see a dome light.

"Hijo de puta." Someone kicked my feet. *"Arriba."*

When the man above me removed his foot, I forced myself to my knees. He opened the side door, got out, and closed it. Someone behind me forced my arms backward and wrapped my wrists together with tape. Whoever it was pulled me by my wrists and pain shot through my shoulders. I moved backward as fast as I could, but not fast enough to avoid more pain. I stumbled from the car and landed on dirt. As I got to my knees, I could hear water as it washed ashore.

"Get up," a harsh voice came from the shadows.

I stood, but almost lost balance. I leaned against the car to steady myself and looked around. There were no lights in the buildings that surrounded me, but the brightness of the moon helped outline them. My eyes didn't want to focus, they stung from the fumes on the floor, and when I squinted, I saw images moving around. I turned toward the back of the car, so I could see where we had come from, and there were streetlights way off.

Someone holding a rifle pushed me away from the car and directed me forward. I walked slowly, my eyes adjusted to the night, and I saw the water between buildings. It was half a football field away and the full moon reflected off the black water.

"*Derecho, derecho,*" the man with the rifle ordered and I turned right.

Someone opened a door, but all there was was blackness, so I hesitated until the rifle poked stiffly into my back. I moved and walked into a dark blanket that moved aside as I continued forward. I smelled kerosene. When I finally pushed my way past the blanket, I was in a room lit with old kerosene lamps. Blackout material covered the windows. Men hurried through the room and entered another. Boxes lined one wall. I was pushed to the middle of the room.

"*Alto,*" the rifle holder ordered.

I stopped. A door closed and then another closed. The rifle barrel hit me aside the head as I went to turn. Someone sat close to the table with the lamp. *Does he understand Spanish?* Someone spoke Spanish behind me. *I think so,* came one answer. *I am not sure,* said another.

I didn't know why it mattered, but I waited. My arms ached and I thought it best that I didn't admit understanding Spanish.

Hit him with your rifle, the person at the table said in Spanish.

I forced myself to relax, because if I tightened up preparing for the blow they would know I understood. The rifle butt hit me hard behind my right knee and I went down, first to my knees, then face to the floor.

Help him up, the man at the table said in Spanish as he stood.

Two men lifted me up by the arms. Pain twisted at my shoulders.

"*Habla el español, Señor Murphy?*" He lit a cigar and I caught a glimpse of his clean-shaven face.

"No," I said and didn't have to fake pain in my voice. "Bar Spanish."

"What is that?" His English was good.

"I can order beer, read items off a menu, get a hotel room, ask where the bathroom is," I kept my voice low.

"And where did you learn this bar Spanish?" The tip of his cigar glowed as he puffed.

"Tijuana, Mexico," I said. "What am I doing here?"

"I was in Tijuana once *Free his hands*," he said in Spanish. "I stood there and stared at America and rode a Mexican helicopter along the border. I was curious about your country."

Someone pulled my arms back and I barked a complaint. I felt a knife cut through the tape on my wrists. When I was untied, I pulled my arms forward and even the pain in my shoulders felt good as I moved freely. I peeled the tape off my wrists.

"You asked to be here." He offered me a cigar.

I took it, bit the end, and he struck a match. I puffed and the flame glowed as the cigar lit. He was in his late fifties, maybe early sixties. He was dressed in civilian clothing, but had a military haircut.

"Thank you, General." I pulled away as the match died.

"Por nada, mi amigo." He dropped the match. "So, now you understand why you are here?"

"I wasn't expecting to meet you here . . ."

"We were surprised to find you in Havana," he cut my words off and motioned toward the table. "And then with a Havana police officer, who takes you to meet with one of our state security people. I was very concerned."

We sat in two old chairs and the odor of kerosene reminded me of the car's floor.

He puffed on the cigar. It helped kill the odor. "Can you explain yourself?"

"Jorge, the cop, he's a cousin of a Key West cop, Luis Morales." I blew smoke toward the lamp, as I made up the lie. "I brought money from Luis' mother for her sister, Jorge's mother."

"And Idania? Do you know her?"

"I never met her before," I said. "I think Jorge was showing her off, so I would tell Luis. He told me she worked for the government, but neither told me what she did. I felt like a third wheel when they asked me to join them, so I left the hotel and was walking back to the Nacional when you had me picked up." Keep mostly to the truth, I repeated to myself.

"But why, at this time, are you in Havana? Why are you not waiting for us to arrive in Key West?"

"Honestly?"

He nodded.

"I don't trust your three men and I don't trust Smith and Jones," I stopped lying. "I thought I could come and see what they were doing on all the trips to the marina. I thought they were lying to me."

"And now?"

"Are you going with them tonight?"

"Yes and the party official. She should be here soon."

"Now I believe them." We both laughed quietly. "It wasn't necessary to kidnap me."

"It was, *Señor*. Never assume people on your side are on your side." He almost smiled in the dimness. "I want you to see where we are. I want you to put all this in your story. This is not about defection, it is about recapturing our homeland from men who are spoiling it with drugs and corruption."

He stood and I followed him to a stack of boxes along the wall. He opened one, pulled a package from it, took it to the table, and unwrapped it.

"This is cocaine." He cut the bag and dumped the white powder. "You see these boxes, they are all full of cocaine. Cuban Communists are using the Colombian cartels to fill their coffers."

He went on for about fifteen minutes, preaching in good English, his plans to save his country. He talked about being

227

tricked in the past by Fidel, the failure of the Communists and the need for a strong military to bring democracy to the country. It was well rehearsed and he wanted to see how it worked on me. I bought the whole package, assured him how it would go in the article and promised him the American public would support such dedication. To put it precisely, he was full of shit.

Now the whole operation was making sense. The three *gusanos* came regularly to Marina Hemingway and smuggled Cubans into the country, but they also brought cocaine, all the while protected by Smith and Jones. How high up did the awareness go? Where did the money go?

I was getting excited about how this article could go when I suddenly realized that Jorge and Idania were preparing to stop the defection. And, it promised to be some battle, judging from the number of armed men I saw moving about.

"Let us walk outside." He was puffed up like a rooster in a henhouse.

A man entered from the inside room and the general excused himself and left me alone. Sitting by myself, smoking a good cigar, I realized I didn't even know his name. The door opened and the general came out, followed by men. Most of the men moved outside, but three stayed with the general.

"*Señor* Murphy, I want to introduce you to three very important men, who are making my plan work." The three men moved next to him. "I have to remember their new names," he laughed. "José Lopez, Carlos Gonzales and Pepe Fernandez."

They stepped forward, I stood and we all shook hands. I hated them and the thin smile on my face may have made them believe I welcomed them, but I smiled because I knew they would all be in a Cuban jail, or dead, by sunrise. José was the man who met me by the dock and asked where he could slip his boat. He was probably the one who knocked me into the water and left me to drown. I fought to keep the images of Michelle

228

and her two friends out of my head.

The general pointed toward the door and we all walked outside.

Armed men patrolled the area. It was an indication that the general had support.

"Where are we?" I looked around at the shadowy outline of high-rise buildings.

"Miramar," the general pointed with his cigar. "These are high-rise apartments being built for Fidel's old friends. They hide cocaine here."

I watched men move boxes onto a go-fast. Maybe they were not using the boat at Marina Hemingway.

"Why are you loading cocaine into the boat?" I moved closer to the general. Two armed men walked behind the five of us.

"Your DEA asked us to bring some with us." He pointed toward the boat. "They can identify where it was made and processed. Once that is known, they can determine what port it left from on its trip to Cuba. Your technology is amazing."

We stopped close to the water.

"Mi General." Pepe put his hand on the general's shoulder to pull him closer.

"Sí Capitán." He put the cigar in his mouth and puffed strongly on it, the tip glowed in the night.

"Why can we not shoot him here and bury him on the beach?" Pepe spoke rapid Spanish, but I understood enough to know the meaning.

The general turned to me, I smiled, and he smiled back. I nervously puffed on my cigar.

"Capitán," he took the cigar out of his mouth, and continued in rapid Spanish. *"Americans have a strange respect for journalists, they love them and they hate them, but they do not kill them. He comes on the boat with us and before we meet the Coast Guard ship you may throw him overboard."* He smiled as he turned to me.

229

"The Gulf Stream will take him toward the Bahamas and maybe the sharks will eat him, but if his body is found it will show no indication of murder. You understand?"

"Sí mi General." Pepe walked away with his two comrades.

"Is there a problem?" I fought my desire to run.

"Pepe is concerned that you have no book or tape recorder for notes," the general lied graciously. "Facts are very important to him, so he is trying to locate some paper."

"I have a tape recorder at the hotel."

"There is not time for that," he said and put the cigar back in his mouth.

A radio squawked from somewhere and a man approached the general.

"Señora Aguero," he said and returned to the shadows.

I caught a brief flash of headlights back behind the building. Someone had come in, but I had an uneasy feeling it wasn't the Marines.

"Prepare to leave, *Señor* Murphy." The general walked away.

The general returned in less than ten minutes with a woman in her mid-fifties, with short-cropped dark brown hair. She looked tired and nervous.

"I hope I will not live to regret this, Rolando," she said in Spanish.

"In a few hours, Maria, you will have wealth and freedom to go along with your beauty," he answered her.

He wanted to introduce her to me, but she would not have it and walked hurriedly toward the go-fast.

"I am sorry," the general said. "She is nervous. A woman, you understand."

"Yes," I smiled but needed a way not to get on the boat. "What about the boat at Marina Hemingway?"

"That will meet us."

"Maybe she would feel better if I went on that boat?"

"She will stay in the cabin." He put his arm around my shoulder as we walked toward the boat. "We will stay on deck. At full speed, we will meet with your Coast Guard in fifteen minutes, maybe less. Do not concern yourself with her."

THIRTY-FOUR

I'm as afraid of dying as the next guy. Getting on the go-fast was certain death, but trying to run in the armed camp that surrounded me was immediate death. I convinced myself that I would fight any effort to toss me overboard; after all, I had the advantage of knowing their plan. But, I held out hope that Jorge and Idania would get there. Men on the aft section of the go-fast started clapping as the general approached and the men that surrounded the dark compound soon followed with applause. Everyone was in civilian clothing, but I had the feeling it was a mixture of enlisted men and officers. Some came up to the general and shook hands, clapped him on the back, wished him luck and a quick return.

The foot of the wood dock was close and we slowed down as the general shook hands and waved to the men who lined the way.

"When I return, *Señor* Murphy," he gloated, "it will be in daylight and as a liberator."

Once you have heard the sound of an incoming round, you never forget it. The general and I stopped at the same time. The applause continued and then the go-fast exploded with a violence that could only have been made by a rocket. The waterfront lit up for a moment and then the boat splinters fell into the water. I can't describe the look on his face; it was a mixture of surprise and determination, not surrender. He was a soldier, a warrior, and this was what his life had been about, battle. His escape was gone and he would die here fighting, or in front of a firing squad. He pulled an automatic from his belt and began yelling orders. I dropped my cigar.

Cuban Guarda Costas boats suddenly appeared off the smoldering dock and heavy machine-gun fire tore up the beach, knocking many to the sandy beach. Bright lights began to beam down from the tops of the surrounding structures and small-arms fire filled the night. Military vehicles blocked openings between the buildings and fired into the compound.

I fell to the sand and lay still. I watched as the mounted machine guns from vehicles tore open the windows and doors of the buildings. Sections began to crumble from a barrage of automatic weapons. Cuban soldiers must have been on the roof, because I saw gunshot flashes in windows on the buildings' higher floors.

The noise was deafening. Slowly, the gunfire dwindled. From one of the military vehicles a loudspeaker amplified orders telling the fighters to surrender. They were told to put down their weapons and stand with their hands locked behind their heads. I'd say it took forever before I saw one man on the beach stand and put his hands behind his head. It was probably less than a minute and then another stood and another. Some helped the wounded up. The dead lay there ruining the white sand.

The loudspeaker ordered them to line up along the water. Some men walked out, but others remained. Small-arms fire continued inside. The loudspeaker ordered them to surrender one more time. No one else came out of the buildings.

Gunfire erupted from the buildings, directed toward the Cuban military vehicles. Cuban soldiers returned fire, machine-gunning the structure, ripping through the exterior. The firing stopped and simultaneously rockets exploded into the two buildings. The ground shook and pieces of the buildings tore away and covered the beach. The noise was loud and fear provoking. Hot chars hit me as I lay on the sand. I reached into my back pocket, pulled out my passport, and hoped it would save me.

The night smelled of cordite, smoke, and death. I stood and placed my hands over my head, with my passport waving in the air. Military vehicles drove onto the beach, and spread out around the buildings. Armed men and women in olive green uniforms moved in, collected weapons and patted down the men lined up at the water's edge. Two soldiers came to me and I handed them my passport. They compared the photo with my face, gave me back the passport, and told me to sit. I obeyed. One stayed with me and the other went to one of the vehicles.

A small team of soldiers entered the burning buildings and two fire trucks pulled up and prepared to put out the fire.

"*Señor Murphy.*" Idania stood over me in a light green shirt and dark green slacks and blackboots, a holster attached to her belt. "Are you okay?"

"Yes. Where is Jorge?"

"Right here." He was dressed in the same two-toned uniform. "I'm sorry about this," he held his hand out to help me stand. I accepted and pulled myself up.

"They were going to dump me into the Gulf Stream." I shook the sand off. "Another five minutes and they would have been gone."

"They were going nowhere," Idania almost smiled. "We were waiting for Maria Aguero."

"That was quick," I said.

They laughed.

"We have had the location and general under observation for some time now." Idania lit a cigarette. "This is a drug operation that your government has been involved in. They would load the go-fast with packages of cocaine and have safe passage into the Keys, sometimes even into Miami."

"Why didn't you tell me?"

"Our informants told us the Miami Cubans spotted you with the *comodoro*, and it panicked them." Idania lit another cigarette off the stub of the one she was smoking. "If we had pulled you out, they would have panicked more. We could not connect General Fuentes and Maria, we needed them together."

"She was on the go-fast that you rocketed," I said. "Do you have the general?"

"We do not know yet." Jorge lit his own cigarette. "Let us take you back to the hotel."

A group of soldiers marched past us. They saluted and I thought I saw Norm in a uniform, smile, wink, and pull at his ear. The ear pull was a greeting we worked out in Mexico, years ago. I shook my head. Even from the back, it looked like him, but I knew there was no way he could be here. Cuba was too dangerous for him.

They kept their word and the news stories had no mention of an American involved in the capture of the general and Communist official. The cocaine scheme discovery was credited to the United States DEA. General Fuentes died fighting, a firing squad would execute the three *gusanos*, and a few other ranking officers before the week was out.

I got to toast Tom one more time with Havana Club Anejo rum as Jorge, Idania, still in uniform, and I stood at the outside bar at the Hotel Nacional, and looked at the full moon reflected off the Gulf of Mexico. I was tired, I was dirty, but I was alive and I couldn't ask for more.

"Has your justice been served?" Idania lit the last cigarette in her package.

I sipped my rum and smoked a cigar. "Yes, but it doesn't bring Tom back or make me feel much better."

"A little better?" She sipped her mojito.

235

"Yes, a little better." I took a long swallow of rum. "I was really scared you were gonna miss me."

"We had people follow you as soon as you left the hotel." Idania blew smoke rings into the night.

"How'd you know they wouldn't kill me at the beach?"

"We did not know." She forced a grin. "But we hoped they would not and we are glad you are alive. I must go." She shook my hand. "If you come back one day, please be a tourist and do not call me." She smiled brightly and left.

"She likes you," Jorge joked. "She's a good person to know in Havana."

"She told me I could have stayed . . ."

"And you could have, she has influence." He raised his glass in a toast. "Tell me about Luis and when you return to Key West tell him about me and that I wait for his visit."

I lied for almost an hour about Luis and his adventures in Key West. We downed a few more drinks, which made lying easier. When Jorge left me outside my room, Luis was the straightest shooter in the whole Keys. He gave me a small envelope and asked me to give it to Luis. I agreed.

I slept until noon Sunday. It was too late to get a flight to Miami, so I met Eddie for a late lunch and told him what happened.

"They have it almost right in the papers," he said after listening to my story. "I checked around for you and then back at the hotel, but no one had seen you."

"It turned out for the best," I toasted him with my Cuban coffee. "I have the afternoon flight tomorrow, can you take me to the airport?"

"Of course." He raised his coffee cup and we clicked.

That evening, after a great afternoon with Eddie and his family, I sat outside the hotel, smoking a cigar, and sipping a rum and Coke when I saw Idania through the large lobby windows.

She walked away from the front desk and came outside.

"Good evening, *Señor.*" She stood and smiled. She wore a colorful dress that stopped above her knees and showed off her legs.

"*Buenas noches, Señorita.* It's nice to see you again." I pointed to the empty seat across from me.

"Can a woman expect a drink from a tired *yanqui?*" She sat next to me.

I saw the waiter staring at her and called him over.

"A mojito for my friend." He nodded his approval and came back quickly with her drink. "Are you working?" We clinked glasses.

"I am always working," she sipped and laughed.

I called Norm from Miami and he met me at the Key West International Airport at midnight.

"I thought you'd be gone." I tossed my bag in the back of the Jeep.

"I haven't left Key West," he said as we drove away. "I wanted to hear your story."

"I swore I saw you on a beach in Cuba."

He laughed. "Yeah, I enlisted." He laughed for the whole ride whenever he looked at me. I never mentioned the military, why did he say enlisted?

I told him what happened and he listened.

"Nothing in the news here," he frowned. "I would like to have seen how the press covered it."

"Not even on CNN?"

"Nope, not CNN or Fox or the other networks."

The marina was dark, and I found a parking spot by the pier.

"You wanna take the Jeep home and pick me up in the morning?"

"Eight o'clock?"

"Sounds about right. Tita . . ."

"I left her here this morning, she said she had some things to do onboard." He drove off.

The *Fenian Bastard* was dark and locked up. Tita wasn't onboard. I went below and there was a note on my chart table.

"Mick, I've gone to visit Paco in Boston. You left me once when I was a kid and told me lies. This time you left me without saying anything. I thought I was part of your life, I know you were part of mine. I guess there are portions of your life I will never understand, never be part of. I don't know if I can handle that. I'm glad you're safe, I worried way too much for you. You are like a sailor chasing the wind and don't realize you will never catch it. I hope you caught your justice and are satisfied. Maybe now, you can put Tom's death behind you and get on with your life. You know where you can find me.

Te amo, Tita."

I flipped the air conditioner on and tossed my bag in the forward cabin. Any man that claims to understand women is a fool or a liar. A cold Mexican Bohemia beer waited for me in the frig. It was good. I went on deck and looked around. So much had happened, but nothing had really changed. The full moon and stars were still in the heavens, the burned-out hull of the yawl remained tied to its dock, it still smelled like smoke, and I was alone.

What would happen now that Smith and Jones' plan failed? Would they come looking for me? Had I committed treason? I was too tired to care. But I did have a good tale to tell at the Hog's Breath.

After all this, nothing had really changed. I wouldn't go to Boston. I wondered if Tita would come back to Key West. I thought about going out on the *Fenian Bastard* and chasin' the wind, something I was good at.

ABOUT THE AUTHOR

Michael Haskins moved to Key West for the sailing more than eleven years ago. He has been the business editor/writer for the daily *Key West Citizen* and the public information officer for the City of Key West. He would rather be chasin' the wind in his sailboat, *Mustard Seed,* but instead, he is working on his next Mad Mick Murphy Mystery, *Free Range Institution.*